Touch Me

AB MONNETTE

Cover Artist : Natchlee Joseph

Formatting: Grace Elena Formatting

To my Wattpad audience. Thank you for dealing with the first drafts and seeing the vision before the product was finished.

Content Warnings

Gunviolence
Talk of sexual assault (the act isn't written, just conversations
about it)
Physically Abuse
Death/murder
Hatecrimes
Use of Drugs and Alcohol

Author's Note

Dear Readers,

Thank you for choosing to read my book *"Touch Me"*. I first started writing this book in 2022 , finishing in 2023. If you're one of my wattpad audience, you will see how far I've come from the first draft. From changing the point of views, and changing the tenses, from having multiple friends read it, editing it by myself for years. And even using Chat GPT to help with the grammar because grammarly wasn't working in my favor (before finding out it was bad for the environment, I do not promote AI, but I'm willing to admit my mistake).

A special shout out to my formattor, @graceelenaformatting (on IG), for being so understanding/flexible, and allowing me to fix some mistakes I missed, because even though I've been editing for 2 years, a lot can still be mixed. If you're a new author, and if you're self-publishing like me, I recommend having her in your corner.

If you don't know me from Wattpad, I recommend checking it out. Although it has its mistakes, my first draft is my baby and I have more books on my profile free for the public(all first drafts).

Touch Me, is Book 1 of my *Love Me Trilogy*. Timeline wise,

it's book 2, the plot will start slow in the beginning, and then pick up. You will be left with some questions, and think "why is this character like this". I promise, all will be revealed. The trilogy is published out of order for a reason, think of it as how Beyonce released Renaissance before Cowboy Carter, when Cowboy Carter was technically written first.

Since the characters in my book are highschoolers, don't expect explicit romance(a.k.a smut). Some characters will get on your nerves, you will see immaturity but remember they are young, their frontal lobe hasn't been developed yet, this is puppy love, childhood romance which will be developed into more in the future. We are growing with the characters, and it will be a beautiful journey.

That's all for now, grab your favorite blanket, cozy up in your favorite reading corner, and enjoy the ride.

With all my love,

A.B. Monnette

Prologue

"Asahi, what did you do?" the woman yelled at the little boy in front of her, tears in his eyes as he looked down at the big man on the ground.

"Mom, I didn't mean to," He cried out, bruises covering his body, his hands shaking in fear. He had just been trying to block the hits, and then he fell, screaming. It was just one touch.

He didn't mean to.

He didn't mean to.

"Get out! You monster, get out!"

"M-Mom, please," he pleaded, but the blonde woman just looked away, her eyes fixed on her husband lying motionless on the floor, her first love.

She looked the adopted help in the eyes.

"I AM NOT YOUR MOTHER. DON'T TOUCH ME!" she screamed as he stepped closer. He froze, then backed away slowly.

"DON'T EVER TOUCH ANYONE, YOU MONSTER! GET THE FUCK OUT!" the woman shouted, the boy stumbled back and ran, bruised and broken, leaving everything behind.

When the police came to retrieve her deceased husband, the

woman told them the boy's biological parents had taken him back a month ago. No one questioned the grieving widow—a high-class woman like her. *What was there to question?*

※ ※ ※

The boy ran. He avoided all human contact and hid for days until someone found him behind a dumpster.

"Honey, there's a child back here," a soft-spoken woman said. She had kinky curls, and her dark skin glowed, even in the rain. Her smile was gentle, motherly.

"Oh, what's he doing here? I'll call the cops," an older man added, eyeing the boy cowering in the shadows. He walked to the side to get better reception.

"Come here, love. What's your name?" the kind woman asked, crouching down to reach him, but he backed away.

"D-Don't touch me," the boy said, voice shaking.

"Okay, I won't," the woman said softly, holding up her hands. Her heart ached for the malnourished, bruised child.

Who could do something so cruel?

"What's your name?" she asked again.

The boy hesitated, then whispered, "A-A-Azrail."

The woman raised an eyebrow at his answer but didn't question it. Instead, she turned to her husband.

"Honey, make sure they bring an ambulance, okay?"

No response.

"Honey?" she called again, louder—but still nothing. Her tone changed. "Come with me," she told the boy gently.

Azrail followed, but kept his distance, trembling from the cold. She handed him her husband's hoodie. He took it carefully, making sure not to touch her.

Then the woman let out a sudden scream. Azrail flinched and backed toward the dumpster, but she wasn't looking at him.

She stared in horror at what lay ahead.

Her husband, beaten to a pulp, was surrounded by two figures, clearly young gang members. Her scream caught their attention. They looked at her and grinned wickedly.

"You killed him," she sobbed in disbelief.

"He wouldn't give us his wallet," one of the men said, grinning with yellow, rotting teeth. "Will you follow directions?"

"L-Leave me alone," the woman begged. Azrail, still trembling, stepped out from behind the dumpster and stood between her and the men.

"Oh, look who's trying to play the hero," one of them said, amused. They both laughed as they towered over him.

"Don't hurt him. He's just a kid."

"Shut the fuck up, bitch," the man snarled, reaching out to slap her—but screamed in pain the moment Azrail caught his wrist.

Pain shot through the man's entire body like electricity. He screeched, then collapsed. The woman and the second man stared in shock as the first lay on the ground, twitching, until he went limp.

"What did you do?" the second man gasped.

Azrail turned to him, touching his glove. The man smirked, thinking the boy's power was gone, but that smirk quickly vanished when Azrail touched his face.

He screamed just like his friend. Then he fell silent.

The woman stood frozen, staring at the boy. Azrail turned to leave, but the sound of sirens stopped him. Red and blue lights flashed as officers poured into the alley.

"What happened?" an officer asked, weapon drawn as he surveyed the scene. Three bodies. One bruised child. One crying woman.

"T-These men came and killed my husband," the woman began, voice trembling, "and hurt my boy. We were just leaving the adoption agency. Before they could get to me, they seized. I think it was the drugs."

Azrail looked at her. She glanced at him with a sharp warning in her eyes—stay silent.

The officer furrowed his brows, unsure. But looking at the scene, the fragile woman, the tiny child, there didn't seem to be a lie in sight.

"Come, we'll take you to the hospital."

"DON'T TOUCH HIM!" the woman shouted, startling both the cop and Azrail. "He's a germophobe. He has a lot of allergies."

The officer nodded, backing off.

As they followed the officer out of the alley, the woman whispered, "One day, you'll tell me your name. And don't worry... your secret is safe with me."

One

AISHA

Just 8 more months and I'll be able to leave.

Just 8 more months.

I repeat those mantras in my mind as I get ready for school. It's the same thing I've been saying to myself since I moved to this small town a month ago.

The same thing I've been saying to forget why I had to move here in the first place.

"AISHA, BREAKFAST!!!!!"

"COMING, MA," I yell back, grabbing my backpack and heading downstairs. I kiss my mom on the cheek and sit down at the table.

My eyes drift to the empty chair across from me and I sigh. As always, my dad's already gone.

"He had an important thing to do at work," Mom says, smiling down at me like that makes it any better.

I just nod. I'm used to not seeing him anyways. I finish my breakfast, grab my keys, and get ready to head out.

"I have practice today so I have to leave early," I tell her. She just nods and waves me off.

On the drive to the studio, I mentally go over everything I've been cramming for that damn calculus test today. As soon as I pull into the lot, I'm out of the car and heading in.

"All right, ladies, let's take it from the top. Aisha, you're late," Coach yells as I walk into the studio.

"Sorry, Coach. Had some trouble in the dressing room," I say, tugging at the tight-ass uniform they gave me.

"We'll make sure to get it altered," she says, waving me off. "Because of your teammate, all of you guys will stay in for an extra hour. We need to be perfect for the performance in December."

Cue the collective groans and the glares aimed directly at me. I roll my eyes and scold myself mentally, I'm definitely going to miss first period now.

"Why didn't you come to first-period today?" Calvin asks as we sit down for lunch.

"Late practice. Where's Jamila?" I ask, biting into my pizza. Coach always tells me to go on a diet, but she can kiss my ass with that. I'm not about to listen to that white bitch.

"In-school suspension for being late too much," Calvin says, not even trying to hide that he's staring at my lips again.

Ever since I moved here, Calvin's had this little crush thing going on, but he's never said anything. I don't exactly come off as the most approachable person. I've been told by him that I give nice hugs, though.

"Damn. Tell me about the new person. Are they hot?" I ask, popping a fry into my mouth while working on an assignment for my last period.

"She's a pretty brunette. Gives off that girl-next-door mixed with nerdy vibes. You guys would get along," he says, his tone honest as he thinks about the new girl he met this morning.

"Mhm," I mutter, eyes back on my work.

"Prof gave her your seat, by the way," he adds just as the bell rings and walks off, leaving me stunned and alone in the cafeteria.

"Now where the hell am I going to sit?" I mumble to myself, quickly packing up and heading out.

❊ ❊

"All right, finish up your stretches and you're free to leave for today," Coach tells us.

While I'm on the floor doing my final stretches, Rosalie plops down beside me.

"Babe, we haven't talked in forever. How are you?" she asks, flashing that big smile at me.

Rosalie's gorgeous—Afro-Latina, confident, and one of the very few Black girls in class. One of the even fewer people I actually let myself get close to. Not on purpose, she just has a likable personality.

"I'm peachy. Just busy with these damn AP classes. Calculus is kicking my ass," I groan.

"Just wait until college. Most of the courses are easier than AP," she says, consoling me. "Doesn't mean you won't hate it less, though."

"Ugh, why can't I just be a housewife?" I complain, flopping down dramatically after finishing my last stretch.

"Because your mom would kill you," she says, and we both burst out laughing.

She's not wrong. My mom's a housewife, and she's already made it crystal clear—I need to get my education first before even thinking about that path.

I never fully got why she hates it so much. Not like I'd ever marry someone like my dad.

"Shit, I'm gonna be late," I curse, giving Rosalie a quick goodbye before rushing to my car. "I don't even have time to fucking change."

I kick off my ballet shoes and swap them for flats before speeding (carefully) down the street. If I'm late again, that's a call to my mom. No thanks.

I fly down the hall and slip into class seconds before the bell rings.

"I see you were able to join us today, Aisha," my professor says with a smirk. "Please sit in the chair in the back row. The new student will sit up front so Calvin can help her catch up."

I shoot Calvin a glare. He just gives me a sheepish smile. And of course, the mysterious new girl everyone's been talking about isn't even here today.

Ignoring the whispers around me, I walk to the back and flop into my new seat. I turn to check out my new seat partner, and stop.

He's dressed in all black, the only skin showing is his face. Pale and seriously handsome, with these piercing brown eyes and jet black hair.

I've seen him before, always sitting in the back. But never this close. He's always the first one in, and no one talks to him. Teachers don't call on him, either. I remember Calvin saying he's a germaphobe, but that doesn't track. Germaphobes usually go out of their way to clean everything before they touch it. He doesn't. His desk is neat, sure, but not obsessively so.

"Hi, I'm Aisha," I say, flashing him a smile, hoping for a proper introduction.

Nothing.

He looks my way briefly, before moving further left, avoiding touching me. I turned my attention back to our teacher, ignoring the embarrassment I felt and the chuckles from my classmates who had witnessed the interaction.

Yeah. Just 8 more months.

Two

AZRAIL

"Azrail, get your ass down here NOW."

My mom's voice hits me like a jolt of lightning. I shoot up in bed, heart pounding, the comfort of sleep shattered. Out of the very short list of things that scare me, my mother sits right at the top—in bold, underlined, highlighted.

"Just a second, Mom!" I yell back, stumbling into the bathroom to wash the sleep off my face. I throw on clothes as fast as I can and rush downstairs. "Yes, Mom."

She's standing at the edge of the kitchen, arms crossed, face set in that expression that makes me feel like I'm nine years old again and just broke something priceless.

"What's this I hear about missing school for a week?"

"Um..." I pause, mind blank, throat tight. "...I love you?"

"Go back upstairs and wash up AND GET YOUR ASS READY FOR SCHOOL NOW."

I'm already halfway up the stairs before she finishes yelling. I don't argue. No point. She's right, I've missed too much. It wasn't supposed to be a week. It was supposed to be a day, maybe two.

But one day off turned into two, then three, and suddenly the whole week was gone. I wasn't trying to be lazy. I just... hate school. Not learning, just school. Too many people. Too much noise.

After finishing up, I make my way back downstairs. She looks at me, her expression softening just a bit, and for a second, I think she might hug me. But of course, she doesn't. Not because she doesn't want to. She can't. The heavens don't allow it.

Finishing my last bite, I stand up, "I'm going to the tattoo shop after-school, bye mom." Blowing her a quick kiss, I ignore the pang in my heart that I can't touch her and walk out.

We live just a few blocks from the high school, so I decided to walk. I think about skipping again, but the thought of my mom's rage pulls me back in line.

When I get to school, I slip on my headphones and walk through the halls like I'm invisible. I've mastered the art of dodging contact. No bumping shoulders. No casual brushes. Nothing.

Ever since freshman year, people have had me pegged. I was the mysterious new guy. Girls were into me. Guys were curious. Then, on day one, a girl reached for my arm and I freaked. Full-on panic. The next day, the principal had a whole damn assembly about my supposed *germaphobia*.

Now, I'm a freak.

I slip into my first-period class and head to my usual spot in the back. A few guys are already there, but no one says anything. No one ever does. That's fine. I lay my head down, hoping to catch a few more minutes of sleep before everything starts.

Then I hear the shuffle, students straightening up, footsteps. The teacher's here. I sit up.

And that's when I see her.

Aisha.

She walks in wearing her usual ballet stuff—tight outfit,

sneakers on. Her presence hits like heat in a cold room. She's quiet too, but where I'm ice, she's fire. Warmth radiates off her.

"I see you were able to join us today, Aisha," the professor jokes.

She walks in confidently, despite the whispers that trail behind her. She throws a glare at her friend—Chris, I think—and it makes me smirk. Those two always seem to be bickering. And for some odd reason, I liked that.

I'm so busy watching her I don't register what the professor says until Aisha starts walking *toward me*.

Wait. No. No, no, no.

Is she sitting next to me?

Yep. She's walking straight over. She doesn't seem phased by the whispers either. That's new.

She sits down and immediately turns to me. I can feel her eyes on my face before I even look.

"Hi, I'm Aisha," she says, smiling like it's the most natural thing in the world. She even extends her hand.

Shit.

I don't say anything. I just stare at her for a second, then her hand. I feel that familiar burn crawl up my spine, the panic. The need to *not* be touched. So I slide left, putting space between us.

A few people chuckle. I glare at them, hard. They shut up quick.

"For your senior project," the professor says, pulling my attention back, "you and your partner will be creating an app. This semester we'll focus on the planning, and next semester you'll collaborate with local college students to build it."

Groans ripple through the class. I stay silent, but internally, I'm screaming.

The professor continues, "Your partners will be your seat mates."

Aisha and I tense up at the same time. Of course. Of course, she's my partner. For the *whole damn year*.

This is going to be hell.

I think, sneaking a glance at Aisha when she wasn't looking.

The rest of the class was like that, silent glances at each other while we barely paid attention to our teacher.

"Alright, you can spend the next ten minutes talking to your partners."

I don't say anything at first. Neither does she. She's focused on her friend, Clark, who's staring at her like she's in danger or something. I roll my eyes. It's not like I'm gonna *kill* her.

Finally, I pull out my phone, slide it to her. "Put your number in. I'll send you updates on the project."

She glares at me, but takes the phone anyway. After sending herself a message, she hands it back.

"I'll be damned if you think you're doing this project by yourself. I'll text you my availability and you text me yours. Then we work with that."

I nod. No argument here. I've worked alone for years, but she clearly isn't going to let that slide.

We sit in silence until the bell rings, both lost in our own heads.

"You sure you don't want someone to tattoo you brother?" The owner of the shop, Jason, says looking me.

"I'm fine Jason."

I've been coming here since I was sixteen, Jason took pity on me. He taught me how to tattoo, I was a pretty fast learner. Now, I'm a regular who tattoos myself and pays Jason for using his supplies. I also occasionally help him with some sketches.

"If you say so, how's school?"

"Good. Nothing new," I lie as I guide the buzzing needle across my skin. The sound calms me like nothing else does.

Jason nods, eyes drifting to my phone which hasn't stopped buzzing for the past minute. He raises a brow.

"That's your mom?"

"No."

"Then who?"

"My partner. For a school project."

Jason smirks. "Since when do you have partners? I thought you always worked alone."

"Yeah, my teacher doesn't care," I mutter. I tried to get out of it. Got threatened with a failing grade.

"So you're just ignoring your partner?"

"She can wait," I say, muting my phone.

Jason suddenly stops what he's doing. "Wait—*she*?"

I look at him.

"You never said it was a *girl*."

"You never asked."

He rolls his eyes. "What's her name?"

"...Aisha."

Jason pauses. "Aisha??? The *new* girl??" He sounds like he's about to explode.

"Yeah."

"And you're not answering her because...?"

"I'm busy."

Jason gives me that look. The one that says *don't test me*.

"Answer her now or I won't let you tattoo here anymore."

I groan, but I unlock my phone. Her texts are stacked up.

AISHA

Hi, it's Aisha. What days and places work for you?

> I'm free all day after school Wednesday, and Friday.

> I'm also free Saturday afternoons, but it'll have to be at my place.

> Can we meet at your place on some days? Or maybe the library? Whichever you're comfortable with.

> If this schedule doesn't work for you we can find a compromise.

> And if we can't meet, we can FaceTime if that's comfortable with you. Or even have a shared document to brainstorm.

She's... considerate.
I type back.

ME

> That works. I'll meet you at your locker after school and we go to my house on the weekdays.

With that answer, I turn my phone off and focus on my new tattoo. Jason, who was peaking over my shoulder, laughs at the interaction.

Three

AISHA

It was Wednesday, and I was late for school again. Not surprising.

But this time, it really wasn't my fault. Well, not *entirely*. I was excited because I heard Dad downstairs. His voice. It had been so long since I heard his voice in the morning like that. I rushed down the stairs, too fast to realize I was skipping the last three. The next thing I knew, I was on the floor.

My mom came running, panic in her eyes before I could even try to sit up. I kept reassuring her, but she wouldn't hear any of it.

She dragged me to the hospital, *three days* earlier than my usual check-up. The doctors, same as always, ran test after test. Full body scans, neuro assessments, the works. And all for two stitches on my foot. Just two. Honestly, it was barely anything compared to some of my past visits.

I have Congenital Insensitivity to Pain. It sounds like a blessing, but it's not. It's terrifying. I can't feel anything, no cuts, no burns, no broken bones.

It was worse when I was younger, I would go a week with a

broken bone and cuts that would go unnoticed until I went to the doctor or until my parents noticed discoloration. I remember the begging I had to do to convince my parents to let me keep dancing, that's how the weekly checkup agreement came to be.

"You missed more than half of the school day today," Jamila said, plopping down next to me.

"I had to go to the hospital," I mumbled while scribbling my unfinished homework.

"Is everything alright?" Calvin asked as he joined us.

"Yup, just fell down the stairs," I shrugged.

"You need to be more careful." There it was, Calvin's lecture voice. Like I hadn't already gotten an earful from my mom this morning.

"I already heard the lecture from my mom. I don't need it from you," I snapped, more out of frustration than anything else. Honestly, I wasn't even mad at him, but I needed someone to direct the day's chaos toward. And to top it off, my dad didn't even stay. He just... left. *Important work*, he said.

Jamila saved us from spiraling into a full-blown argument. "Why didn't you just miss the whole day? You would've had more time to finish your work."

"I have an appointment after school," I said quietly, trying to stay focused.

"With who?" Jamila tilted her head.

"Azrail. I'm going to his house to work on our project."

"You're going to his house? Why not in the library or something?" Her voice jumped two octaves. I just shrugged.

Calvin stayed silent. That said enough. He had *opinions*, clearly.

"He tried to do the project himself, but I told him no."

Jamila kept staring, and I hated that look. I knew she wasn't judging, just surprised, but still. I got defensive. "Just be careful. He's a freak," Calvin muttered finally, voice tight.

I rolled my eyes. "And how would you know that? He just doesn't talk to people. He doesn't like being touched. That's a healthy boundary, if you ask me."

"She's right, Calvin," Jamila chimed in, trying to keep the peace. "And Aisha, maybe be a little nicer."

We both muttered half-hearted apologies and dropped it. No point in arguing.

❀   ❀

Later that day, I stood by my locker, checking my phone. Still nothing from Azrail.

"Where is he?" I asked aloud.

"Maybe he thinks you're not here today since you missed first-period," Calvin said.

"That's why I *texted* him this morning."

Just as I was about to call, I saw his familiar figure. Azrail as always was in all black, this time he was also wearing a mask only his eyes and hair were visible. I stood straighter instinctively.

"Ready?" he asked, and I swear my heart did something weird. First time I'd ever heard his voice.

I nodded, said goodbye to my friends, and followed him.

"I didn't bring my car today, so can I ride in yours?"

"I walk to school," he said, rolling his eyes when I struggled to keep up.

Oh. Okay. Guess we were walking.

"Why were you late? Didn't you get my messages?"

He stopped. Just looked at me. Intense, unreadable. Then he pointed to the other side of the sidewalk.

"Get over here," he said. "I saw your messages. I was just busy."

I kept my head down. "Oh."

The silence after that wasn't awkward. It was… comfortable.

His house wasn't far. When we got there, he told me I could sit in the kitchen and disappeared upstairs.

I took out my notes, waited. When he sat on the opposite side of the table, I rolled my eyes, picked up my stuff, and moved next to him.

"Look, I know you don't like being touched. I'll respect that. But for the love of my grades, please cooperate."

He nodded. Quiet, as always.

Eventually, we got to work. "So what kind of app do you think we should create?" I asked, flipping through Calvin's notes, not that they helped much.

Azrail handed me his notebook. His handwriting, his sketches... they were *insane*. I gasped.

"You're very good. Ever considered becoming an artist?"

He blushed, then showed me his tattoos. "I like tattooing."

"That's pretty cool. Oh, I love that buttefl-" I almost reached for it but caught myself when he flinched. "Sorry. Your tattoos are cool. You shouldn't hide them."

"We should design an app that's useful but also not hard to create," Azrail says, changing the topic. I get the hint and nod. "What about something school-related?"

"That sounds a bit boring, and also a lot of people might try to do that for an easy A."

"Don't we want an A?" Azrail asks in confusion.

"We want an A+," I corrected. "What about a video game?"

"Too complex, plus he said our app has to be educational."

"Ugh."

Three hours passed. We still had no solid idea. My phone rang.

"Hi, Ma."

"It's getting late young lady, make your way home." Her voice was stern. Time to go.

I apologized and packed up. "Can't believe it's been three hours. I still have to study for calculus."

"How are you getting home?" Azrail asked.

"I'll just walk."

He looked skeptical, but didn't argue. Just walked me to the door.

"Um, well… see you when I see you," I said, awkward as ever.

He nodded. Closed the door.

By the time I realized how dark it had gotten, it was too late. I should've called someone. The wind picked up. I wrapped my jacket tighter.

Then I heard him.

"What's a young lady like you doing in the dark?"

My blood ran cold.

I tried to walk away, staying polite. It didn't work. He grabbed me. I screamed. Fought back. He slammed my head into the wall. I didn't even feel it, only knew by the impact.

"Please… stop," I begged.

He noticed I wasn't reacting. "What are you, a freak or something?"

Then, a voice: "She said, let her go."

Azrail.

The man turned to him. He tried to fight him. The second his fist connected with Azrail's face, he *screamed*. Loud. Blood-curdling.

Then…darkness.

Four

AZRAIL

When I didn't see Aisha in the first half of the day, I thought maybe she finally decided she didn't want to deal with me. That would've been fine. Preferable, even.

But then she texted me. More than once. Persistent, like always.

I didn't respond.

Didn't mean I wasn't going to meet her. Just... needed time to get my mind right.

When I saw her by the locker, waiting with her friends, my stomach twisted. She stood up straighter when I got closer.

"Ready?" I asked.

She nodded, said her goodbyes and followed me.

"I didn't bring my car today, so can I ride in yours?"

"I walk to school," I replied, picking up my pace. She struggled to keep up.

I hoped she'd cancel. I'd left her messages unread on purpose. But of course, she had to show up.

"Why were you late? Didn't you get my messages?"

I stopped and looked at her. She was too close to the road. I pointed her to the safer side.

"Get over here. I saw your messages. I was just busy."

She didn't push. Just nodded.

At the house, I told her to wait in the kitchen. I needed a minute. I needed to make sure everything was covered. The sleeves, the gloves, the mask. All of it.

Just a few hours. Then she'll leave.

Back downstairs, I tried to sit far away. Of course she dragged her chair over.

"Look, I know you don't like people touching you and I will respect that, but for the love of my grades, please co-operate."

She didn't back down.

I nodded, not saying anything to her. For such an innocent-looking person, she was tough. I noticed the way she hit her side on the table and didn't react, but I ignored.

When I saw her struggling to understand her friend's notes, I handed her mine. Careful not to touch her. She gasped at the doodles.

"You're very good. Ever considered becoming an artist?"

I didn't know how to respond. Instead, I showed her some old ink. She reached for it, then pulled back. She caught herself. That... surprised me.

"You shouldn't hide them," she said. Then she dropped it.

We brainstormed. Disagreed a bit. Hours passed. It felt weirdly easy. She was annoying, but also, motivated. Unfiltered. Honest.

Her phone rang. Time was up.

"How are you getting home?"

"I'll just walk."

I didn't like that answer. But I let her go.

❦ ❋ ❦

I don't understand what the hell is wrong with me.

The second the sun started going down, I got uneasy. Told myself it was just the usual itch to walk outside and smoke. But deep down, I knew it was about *her*.

I told myself I was just going out for a smoke.

Then I heard her scream.

The moment I turned the corner and saw that bastard with his hands on her, something snapped in me. And the weirdest part? She wasn't screaming from pain. She didn't *react*. Not when he hit her. Not when he threw her against the wall. Nothing.

It wasn't normal.

I didn't plan to kill him. I just wanted to knock him out.

But he swung at *me*. And I didn't move fast enough. Or maybe I didn't want to.

He touched me.

He screamed.

She fainted.

I stood there, breathing hard. I didn't know what to do. I wanted to help her—pick her up, take her to the hospital—but I knew I couldn't. So I called the one person I always call.

"Hi sweetie, I'm almost home. What's up?" Mom answered instantly.

"I need you to make a quick stop," I muttered, eyes fixed on the mess in front of me.

She arrived in five minutes flat.

I told her everything. She didn't ask too many questions. Just… handled it. Told me to sit in the car, called the cops, and gave them her version: she'd seen the guy dragging Aisha into the alley, and by the time she got there, the girl had fainted.

The pervert's death was ruled an overdose.

Just like that.

Now I'm in the hospital, sitting in a chair in her room. Watching her sleep. I don't even know why I came.

"She got attacked while walking home," my mom said calmly as Aisha's mom walked in, panicked and crying. "Nothing grave happened before we found her. Mild concussion."

Her mom stared at me. I stood up. "Azrail. We were working on a project at my house. Sorry for not making sure she got home safe."

She didn't buy the lie, not fully. But she gave me a nod anyway. "Thank you."

When we left, Mom said nothing until we got to the car.

"She'll most likely miss at least a day of school. Make sure you give her the missing work," she said.

I nodded and went to my room. But I couldn't stop thinking about it.

Why didn't she flinch?

※ ※ ※

The next day, some loudmouth kid stood in front of my locker asking questions.

"Azrail, what happened to Aisha?"

I ignored him.

"I saw you going to teachers and getting her homework—what happened?"

"Move out of my way, Chris."

"My name is Calvin."

Didn't care.

I grabbed my stuff and left. I was driving today. First time in a while. I hated driving, but it was faster.

At the hospital, Jesse smiled when she saw me.

"Just go on up," she said. "Her mom left an hour ago, and her dad's due in thirty."

I nodded and took the stairs.

When I got to her room, she looked… intense. Books and paper everywhere. Like she was trying to bury herself in it.

She looked up when she heard me.

"Dad—oh. Hi."

"Hi," I said. "I, um, brought your homework."

"Thanks. Come in."

"You didn't miss much. Reading test tomorrow, calculus on Monday."

She groaned. Slammed her head back.

"Sorry, it's just that studying isn't my strong suit. Missing a day ruins everything for me."

I nodded. Then the words left my mouth before I could stop them.

"I could help you. If you want. I took that class last year."

"Thanks for the offer… but I'm a terrible student. No one ever teaches me in a way I understand."

"I'll take my chances."

We stared at each other for a while.

Then I said it.

"What are you?"

She looked confused. "Huh?"

"I'm sorry," I said. "It's just… I saw what he did, and you didn't even flinch."

"What about you? I saw what *you* did."

"Touche."

She told me everything. About her disorder. About how she can't feel pain. About the checkups, and how it might shorten her life.

I listened.

Before I could say more, her dad came in. She runs to him and jumps into his arms, while he stays stills.

Tall. Stern. Cold.

"Um, I just came to check if you were okay. It looks like you are, so I'll be going. Work at the office and all."

She just nodded.

After he left, I saw the tear she tried to hide.

I wanted to say something. So I said the dumbest thing.

"Um… also your boyfriend asked about you. I told him you were in the hospital."

"Boyfriend?? Who??"

"Kade."

"Kade? I don't know any Kad—oh you mean *Calvin*?"

I shrug.

She laughed. "Calvin isn't my boyfriend. I turned off my phone to study. I'll make sure to text him soon."

"Oh, you have a lash on your cheek," She reached towards me. Touching my cheek.

I didn't expect it.

And I didn't pull back in time.

Both of us froze.

Oh shit.

Five

AISHA

When I woke up, machines were beeping around me. Mom was there. Crying, hugging me, worried sick.

"You're finally awake," she said, pulling me into a hug.

I just held her, letting her fuss over me. "Next time call me, call an Uber, call *somebody*, never walk home alone in the dark again."

"Sorry ma," I said quietly. "I thought I was going to make it before it got dark."

She told me what the doctors had said, just bruises and a mild concussion. Honestly? Not bad, considering.

"When can I leave?" I asked.

"Tomorrow night. They just want to monitor you."

I nodded and leaned back, mentally calculating all the things I was going to miss. Practice. Calculus exam. Homework.

"So, Azrail?"

"Huh?" I blinked. *How does she know about him?*

"He and his mom brought you here. Cute boy."

I felt my face heat up. *Azrail* brought me here? *Why?*

"Ma, can I get my bag, please? I need to catch up on schoolwork."

She frowned. I could tell what she was thinking. That I was throwing myself into school again like I always do after something bad happens.

"You're sure, sweetie? You took a pretty big blow to your head."

"Can't feel anything, remember?" I said with a knock to the head and a laugh. She didn't laugh back, just looked at me like I was made of glass.

But she gave me my stuff. I got to work. Numbers were easier to deal with than people.

I don't know how long passed before I heard someone clear their throat.

"Dad—?" I looked up, expecting the one person I hadn't seen yet. But it wasn't him.

"Oh. Hi," I said, surprised. Azrail stood there awkwardly, holding something in his hand.

"Hi," he said. "I, um, brought you your homework."

"Um, thanks. Come in," I said, gesturing.

"You didn't miss much," he said, stepping inside. "But there is a reading test tomorrow, and another calculus test Monday."

"Fuck," I groaned, falling back onto the bed. I squeezed my eyes shut, trying to hold in the tears. "Sorry, it's just that studying isn't my strong suit. Especially calculus. Missing a day ruins everything for me."

He nodded. Didn't say anything for a bit.

Then he surprised me.

"I um... could help you. If you want. I took that class last year."

I blinked. *Azrail offering help?*

"Thanks for the offer," I said slowly, "but I gotta warn you. I don't do well with tutoring. No one ever explains things in a way I understand."

"I'll take my chances."

I smiled at that. We looked at each other in a moment of awkward silence before he said something unexpected.

"What are you?"

I blinked. "Huh?"

"I'm sorry," he muttered, shaking his head. "It's just that I saw what the perv did and... you didn't even flinch."

I looked him straight in the eye. "What about you? I saw what *you* did."

"Touche."

We both fell quiet again. I finally told him the truth.

"I have a disorder that makes me immune to pain. I have no sensation of external injuries. Can't feel if I'm burning or freezing, etc."

He just listened. Didn't interrupt.

"It seems cool at first," I said, "but it also lowers my lifespan. I could get injured and not notice until it's too late. So I'll be going to the doctor once a week for the rest of my life."

Azrail was still quiet when the door opened again.

"Oh, sorry. I didn't realize you had company," a deep voice said.

"Daddy!!" I jumped up before I could think better of it, rushing into his arms.

He hugged me stiffly. His face was unreadable, like always.

"Um, I just came to check if you were okay. It looks like you are, so I'll be going. Work at the office and all."

I just nodded. I was used to the excuses by now. But it still hurts.

When he left, I turned my face away so Azrail wouldn't see me wipe the tears.

Then, he spoke again.

"Um, also your boyfriend asked about you. I told him you were in the hospital."

"Boyfriend?? Who??"

"Kade."

"Kade?" I said, confused. "I don't know any Kad—oh you mean *Calvin*?"

He shrugged. I laughed.

"Calvin isn't my boyfriend. I turned off my phone to study. I'll make sure to text him soon."

Azrail nodded. Then something strange happened. He looked at me, *really* looked, and I saw something on his cheek.

"Oh, you have a lash on your cheek," I said, reaching toward him.

The moment my fingers brushed his skin, he froze.

So did I.

Oh shit.

Six

AISHA

Oh shit.

My hand was still in the air. His skin still warm on my fingertips.

The room was dead silent, like the whole world paused to see what would happen next. I could hear my heart beating in my chest. Fast. Loud. Almost as if it didn't trust me to breathe on my own.

I didn't mean to touch him. It was a reflex. A habit. I always did that when someone had a lash on their cheek. Something my mom did to me when I was younger. But this wasn't just anybody.

This was Azrail.

❀   ❀

AZRAIL

I held my breath the second her fingers brushed my cheek. Everything in me screamed *back away*, but I couldn't move. I just stood there, waiting… for something. For *anything*.

But nothing happened.

She didn't scream.

I didn't black out.

The air didn't explode with pain or curses.

Nothing.

Aisha let out a breath, soft and slow. Relief.

"I, um… I have to go. See you tomorrow," I muttered, stepping back before I could unravel right in front of her.

I left before she could say anything.

Got in the car.

Drove home.

Ran upstairs.

Didn't even glance at Mom.

Everything inside me was burning. My chest was tight. My lungs felt like they were collapsing.

I was having a panic attack.

"Azrail, what's wrong??" My mom's voice cut through the chaos. She was in the room in seconds, wide-eyed, panicking herself.

"Mom, I—I can't breathe—" My vision was blurring, my body overheating. I couldn't think.

She didn't touch me, just got close enough to talk me down. She coached me through breathing, grounding, her voice calm and steady. Like she'd done before. Years ago.

It took time, but eventually the shaking stopped. My chest stopped screaming.

Later, she brought me food and told me to stay home from school. I didn't argue.

But I also didn't tell her anything.

Not about the touch.

Not about Aisha.

Not about how a part of me *wanted* it to happen just to see if she was truly immune. Or if my curse was evolving. Or if I was just losing it.

None of this made sense.

Why was this girl making everything so… *complicated?*

🐢 🐢

AISHA

He didn't show up Friday.

Didn't text.

Didn't call.

Didn't show up Saturday either.

Twice I tried to reach out. Twice he canceled. I told myself not to be hurt, I *had* crossed a boundary. I touched him without asking. I get it.

But it's Tuesday now.

Still nothing.

I was sitting at lunch with Jamila and Calvin, but they were wrapped in their own little conversation about some new girl I hadn't met.

So I cut in.

"What do you guys know about Azrail?"

That shut them up.

Jamila blinked. Calvin stared at me. I tried to look casual.

"Nothing much," Jamila finally said. "He and his mom moved here freshman year."

"Has he ever missed this many days?"

"Yeah, he disappears sometimes. I don't know why. Still somehow keeps his grades up. Why the sudden curiosity?"

I shrugged. "Just curious about my partner. If I want to pass, I need to make sure the project gets done."

Jamila nodded, buying the excuse. Calvin didn't look so convinced.

"So," I said, pivoting fast, "has he ever dated?"

Jamila gasped and clapped her hands together. "OHMYGOSH, YOU *TOTALLY* HAVE A CRUSH ON HIM!"

I reached over and covered her mouth, mouthing "sorry" to the people nearby she'd disturbed. My cheeks burned, but I forced a grin.

"No. Just curious."

"That freak's never dated," Calvin said coldly. "Stay away from him. He's bad news."

Jamila and I both shot him a glare.

"Ignore him," she said, waving Calvin off. "He might just be shy. I say go for it, just be careful. Plus, you two would be *so* cute together."

I didn't respond.

I didn't need to.

My embarrassed face says it all.

After school, I went to his house.

I knew it was probably overstepping. Jamila told me his disappearing act was normal. But... I couldn't shake the worry.

I rang the doorbell.

No answer.

Rang it again.

Still nothing.

Just as I turned to leave, the door opened. His mom stood there, hair wet, shirt damp, probably just finished washing it.

"Sorry for coming unannounced, ma'am. I have Azrail's missing work from school."

She smirked like she didn't buy it at all, but she let me in anyway.

"Upstairs. First door on your right," she said. "I'd tell him he has a guest, but that would just make him run."

I laughed nervously, kicked off my shoes, and headed up.

I knocked once.

"Come in, Mom."

His voice caught me off guard.

I opened the door slowly and stepped inside.

He was lying on his bed, back to me. Plain green shirt. Black sweats. Still. Quiet.

"Your mom said it was okay for me to check on you," I whispered.

He jolted upright when he saw me, startled.

"I'm sorry to intrude," I said quickly, walking further in. "I just wanted to check up on you. I'll leave soon. I know we aren't friends or anything, and I did kind of take up your personal space. Sorry about that. People say you usually miss school sometimes, and I know it's none of my business, especially since you still keep your grades up or whatever, but I just wanted to make sure you were okay. I'm rambling. I'll just shut up now."

My eyes landed on a stuffed turtle sitting on his dresser. It was cute.

He noticed.

"My mom gave it to me," he said suddenly. "I used to have nightmares. Since she couldn't touch me, she sprayed it with her perfume so I could hug it and sleep. She said it would help me get out of my shell."

He smiled faintly at the pun. I smiled too.

"Then why is she over there?" I teased. "She should be sleeping next to you every night."

I walked over, picked it up, and gently tossed it toward him.

He didn't catch it. It fell on the floor.

"What, um…" He cleared his throat. "What did you feel when you… when you touched me?"

I smiled, heart beating a little too fast.

"I felt warm," I said softly. "Not physically, but emotionally. It felt… nice."

He nodded.

Didn't say anything for a while.

Still wouldn't look at me.

So I sat down on the bed beside him.

"I don't really get affection from my dad," I admitted, picking the stuffed animal up. "So I tried to find other ways. My health-iest outlet became my stuffed animal collection. I have so many, they take up my room. So believe me when I say, take care of Ms. Turtle. They all deserve love."

I tossed it back to him. This time, he took it.

He actually *laughed*.

And God, it was worth everything.

Then he spoke.

"When I was young… something happened to me. I was cursed. Everyone, anything alive, that comes in contact with my skin feels so much pain it kills them."

I blinked.

Sat there in silence.

He didn't look at me.

Didn't want to see my reaction.

"It's funny, really," I said, breaking the quiet. "A girl who can't feel pain and a boy who inflicts it. Paired up by some random teacher."

Azrail chuckled.

"The angel of death with life. I wonder what could happen," He added, smiling at the poetic irony of our names.

I laugh.

He looked at me then, eyes dark but soft. "Are you bold enough to find out?"

My heart skipped.

"Touch me and we'll see."

Seven

∽

AZRAIL

"Touch me and we'll see." Her words leave me stunned.

I moved my finger closer to her, the silence was deafening. The tension in the room was suffocating. Both of our minds are racing with the same thought.

What if last time was just luck and something happens this time?

Finally, I allow my pinky to touch her, she lets out a small gasp and I pull away looking at her.

"Is something wrong?" I quickly ask, worried that I just signed her death certificate.

Aisha shakes her head, her chest going up and down as she breathes. "Sorry, I forgot how to breathe for a second."

I look at her dumbfounded while she just smiles at me. "Stop being so scared,"

She grabs my hand with hers and I try to pull away but she stops me. "See, nothing is happening."

"Yeah, nothing."

We both stay quiet, not breaking eye contact. "Feels nice doesn't it," She gestured at our interlocked hands.

I nod. The warm feeling was extremely comfortable. I never realized how much I missed skin-to-skin contact until now.

"C-can we stay like this?" I stutter out, my cheeks heating up when the words leave my mouth.

Before I could take it back, she nodded. "Let's make it better, lay back."

I gulp and follow her direction. I lay back on the bed and watch her actions, already missing the warmth from our hand holding.

She gets on the bed and lays her head on me. I watch her take my hand and put it around her. When she's done adjusting us, she looks up at me and gives me a big squeeze.

"Let's cuddle."

I nod. Too scared to say anything, enjoying the interaction.

AISHA

My phone ringing wakes me up. I groan, searching around and picking up. "Hello."

"Hi honey, did I wake you up?"

"Hi ma, whats-up."

"Just checking to make sure you ate, I'm staying in the city with your father today so I won't be coming home till tomorrow morning."

"Okay, I'll go get something to eat now," I mumble. We say our goodbyes and I focus on the warm body next to me and try to go back to sleep.

Wait.

My eyes open and I look at the chest in front of me.

I quickly moved back and gasped, Azrail was still sleeping next to me and by the looks of it our body was intertwined pretty nicely. I let out a sigh of relief when I noticed we were both wearing clothes, and the memories of what happened early rushed back to me.

I thought I did something stupid again.

I gather my stuff and make my way out of his room, giving the sleeping boy one last glance before closing the door. I make my way out the door to put on my shoes.

"Leaving so soon?" The voice of Azrail's mom makes me drop my phone. "Sorry dear, I didn't mean to startle you."

"Sorry, I didn't mean to fall asleep." She shakes her head at my apology and takes my hand.

"It's alright dear, you guys looked peaceful and it's nice seeing that Azrail met someone like you." I nod, understanding the weight of her words. I am the only one able to touch Azrail for some reason.

"I'll be leaving now," I mutter. "Thank you for your hospitality."

"Nonsense, eat something first, and then you could leave." His mom says, taking my hand and dragging me to the dining room.

I look at the plates in front of me and nod. Her food looks delectable, I'm definitely staying now.

"Dear, plug your ears for a second please." She says and I follow her strange request.

"AZRAIL DINNER," I flinch at her voice. For someone so soft-spoken, she had some base in her voice.

She sends me an apologetic smile and soon enough, her son is in the dining room. His hair was all over the place and he looked like he was trying to make sense of the world. He looks at me and I quickly look down, feeling my face warm up.

"Sit and eat." His mom says, pulling the chair next to me.

I don't look up when he sits next to me, I just focus on the food in front of me.

"So are you guys dating?"

The question sends both of us on a coughing spree. I take the water and drink it.

"Mom," Azrail mutters embarrassingly. I looked at him and saw that he was blushing.

"What, I went to check on you guys and I saw the cutest thing." She says, showing us her phone. It was Azrail and I cuddled. His head on my chest and my arm wrapped around him securely. Azrail turns scarlet at the picture.

"We aren't dating." I finally speak up, trying to save us both.

"Aisha was the only one I can touch without hurting, things happen, and I guess we fell asleep," Azrail explains to his mom.

She nods but still has a smirk on her face looking at us, "Alright, eat and I'll stop teasing."

"Sorry about that," Azrail whispers when his mom walks away.

I nod, "It's okay, sorry for not leaving sooner."

"I don't mind, I was more disappointed when I didn't see you."

Now it was my turn to blush even more.

Good thing mine is not visible.

Eight

AISHA

"**D**addy, are you still coming to my performance next week?"

"I have a meeting at that time sweetheart."

I quickly hid my frown with a smile, "But I didn't even tell you the time?"

I watched him freeze for a second before looking at my mother who was scowling at him. "I'll be busy all day."

I nod and say nothing else.

Feeling my throat closing up I get up from the table not finishing my breakfast.

"I just remembered that I need to get to class early for a project," I mutter, picking up my bag. "Bye daddy, bye ma."

I left the house before they could say anything. Thankful that my mom didn't force me to finish breakfast like she normally would.

The moment I got to the car, I let my tears fall.

Why couldn't I be immune to emotional pain?

I got to my first-period class earlier than usual. The only person in the class was the twins that I've never talked to and Azrail. I sat next to him, careful to not bother him since his head was down.

Things were weird, and I don't know if it was a good or bad thing. The last time we saw each other was two days ago during the napping incident.

I think about hugging him all the time, but I don't want to make him uncomfortable. So I say nothing, waiting for him to make a move but that still hasn't happened.

"Is the world ending?"

I'm pulled out of my thoughts by his voice. I look at him and raise a brow. He was still laying on his desk and glancing up at me.

"What?"

"The world must be ending if you're in class early."

I roll my eyes at his words, a smile sneaking its way on my lips. "No, I just don't have morning practice today."

"Even when you don't have morning practice, you're here on time, not early." He points out. I nod agreeing with his observation.

"Just wanted to leave the house," I mumble, remembering what happened this morning. "My dad isn't coming to my performance next week."

He nods in understanding. He is the only person that knows about my relationship with my father, I don't even know why I told him. It just felt right.

"When's your performance?"

"Next Thursday evening," I tell him, getting excited. "It's a small performance to get people ready for the end of year one."

"That sounds fun, how long have you been dancing?"

"Since I was two, I loved dancing and was determined. I want to make it national one day."

"Do you want me to-"

"What are you doing here so early?" Calvin's voice cuts Azrail off.

Azrail rolls his eyes and lays back down and I go back to Calvin, kind of irritated that he interrupted us.

"I'm failing the class, I can't afford to be late." I half lied.

He nods believing me. "I won't be able to come to your performance next week."

I frown, not him too.

"Why not? You promised."

"Sorry, the girl I told you about. She needs help catching up on her classes since she missed so many days and started the school year late."

"Okay, whatever."

My irritation levels were starting to rise more and more. I still haven't met this so-called girl and she has Calvin whipped. I have a bad feeling about this new girl.

"I want you to meet her, she's coming today." He says gushing about her. "You'll love her."

I nod and before I could say anything someone walks into the room.

No, it can't be.

"There she is," Calvin says smiling, while I feel the color drain from my face.

Maybe she has a twin.

"Abbey, come meet the friend I told you about."

It was her.

I watch as the brunette walks up to us and smiles at Calvin who put his arm around her. She sends me one of her record-breaking fake smiles.

"Hi."

I nod and say nothing. Clenching my jaw.

"Sorry, she's sort of an introvert at times." Calvin excuses my behavior and I glare at him. Why is he talking about me like I'm a pet?

"Cain, you're interrupting my rest, talk to your friend after class." I looked at Azrail who was glaring at Calvin.

"It's Calvin." Calvin was also glaring. The tension between them was deadly.

"We can talk later, Calvin." I cut in, not liking the attention the boys were giving.

I watch as Abbey drags Calvin to their seat. She hasn't changed, still the same sweet innocent-looking girl. Blushing every time Calvin says something and Calvin eating it up every damn time.

I feel a hand on my knee, stopping it from bouncing. I look at Azrail who gave me a questioning look, I smile in return. He interlocked his fingers with mine and leaned close to my ears.

"Let's focus before you fail." He whispers as the teacher walks into the room. I nod, enjoying the calming effect the hold had on me.

❀ ❀ ❀

AZRAIL

I hate that Ben.

I noticed how he was always looking down at Aisha's shirt and her lips every time he talked to her.

He had no respect for her as a friend, he didn't have a crush. He just sexualizes her.

And to make it worse, he isn't attending an event that's important to her for another girl.

It bothers me how much Aisha allows Jake to affect her. I think back to her irritation in class when he introduced her to that new girl, I don't even know why I grabbed her hand, it just felt right.

It's now lunch and I'm in the corner eating the biohazard the school serves us, and looking at Aisha's table.

At first, she was with Jamila and they were having fun until Chris came with Abigail, soon enough the table was filled with different people talking to everyone but Aisha. She looked irritated and I noticed the smug look Abigail was giving her.

Aisha starts to look around the lunchroom, probably trying to find a distraction. When her eyes land on me, her face lights up and she gestures outside the lunchroom. I raise a brow at that but nod anyway.

I watch her give her friend Jamila an excuse before leaving the cafeteria and after a few minutes, I follow her and walk out. She was leaning on a locker, waiting for me.

"You called?" I ask, raising a brow.

"You were staring." She points out before walking up next to me.

"And you were searching."

"Touché," She lets out a chuckle. I smile at the angelic sound. "Can I get a hug?"

I nod, pulling her into a hug. Smiling at the contact.

I used to think I would be fine without human contact since it's been so long but meeting Aisha changed that. Now I'm addicted to her hug.

"Want to talk about it?" I ask, not pulling away. Enjoying the contact between us.

"We used to be old friends." She answers, knowing exactly what I was talking about.

"Mhm."

"Want to skip?"

"I have a calculus test tomorrow and I need the review." She mumbles on my chest, not letting go.

"I can tutor you."

"You can try," She laughs leaning back slightly to look up at me, her hand still around me. "I told you I'm difficult."

"Come on, I'll walk you to class," I mutter, ignoring how fast she makes my heartbeat.

"Are you still skipping?" She asks as we interlock our fingers and make our way to class.

"Yes, I got nothing to learn anyways."

She rolls her eyes and mocks me. "Lucky bitch."

I let out a small laugh. We stay silent in front of the class-room, smiling and not letting each other go.

The bell rings and brings us out of our daze.

"See you tomorrow?"

"Bye Sunshine," I say, giving her a kiss on the cheeks and walking away before the hallway gets piled up.

This girl is going to be the end of me.

Nine

AISHA

"I know what app we can do for our project," Azrail says out of nowhere, letting out a puff of smoke.

It's Saturday and my parents aren't home, as usual. After a rigorous practice and failing my Calculus test yesterday Azrail came up with a good idea of getting high to relax.

"What?" I mumble eating my vanilla ice cream, feeling incredibly relaxed.

"An app that helps you study, via games." He says, passing me the blunt.

I hum, taking a deep breath. I haven't smoked in months, and never liked it, but something about doing it with Azrail makes it fun.

"And you can be the test subject, try to see if it'll help you with Calculus." He continues taking the blunt back from me.

"An app to help me pass classes, yes sir," I mumble sliding down the couch and giggling.

"We can call it, Studyella or some shit."

"Um, what about Athena?" He suggests. "She is also the goddess of wisdom."

"Nah, too basic," I mutter. "What about Paideia, it's the Greek word for 'education' and it looks pretty."

"Not many people can pronounce that," Azrail points out.

"Ugh," I groan, laying down wanting to cry.

"Why don't we take a break," Azrail suggests. I nod and take my blanket and snuggle next to him.

"Nap time." I squeal, laying on his chest and bringing him into a big hug.

"What about your parents?" He says, chuckling.

"They won't be back till Monday, now shush and cuddle."

I smile, enjoying the vibration on his chest when lets out a laugh.

❦　❦

Rosalie is freaking out and I'm trying to calm her, but how the fuck can I do that when I'm freaking out too.

"Rosalie, calm down, you are going to do amazing," I say for the umpteenth time.

"I want to do more than just amazing, he's watching me perform today." Rosalie gushed, talking about her crush who's here to watch the performance.

Rosalie was getting tattooed by him and casually mentioned the concert and he invited himself to come and watch, and now that he's here she can't sit still.

"When he sees you dance, he will be head over heels." Ally, our makeup artist says, putting on the finishing touches on Rosalie's face.

"The way he invited himself, he's already head over heels." I tease taking a few selfies, trying to forget the fact that no one is coming to see me. Jamila is grounded because of the amount of classes she missed,, unlike me, she doesn't have an excuse, and Calvin is with *her*. Father is doing whatever he pleases and I told mom that she didn't need to come because I would feel worse.

Maybe I should've invited Azrail.

"Shut up, you think so?" Rosalie gushes, and I nod.

"Alright ladies, get in position." Coach instructs and we all move to our assigned roles.

Alright, Aisha. Deep breaths, big smiles, you are going to do amazing.

The start of the music concluded my pep talk.

The lights shined on us, and the curtain rises.

Show time.

AZRAIL

I watch her move flawlessly across the stage. The way she dances so passionately as if dancing is easier than breathing to her.

She was in the middle and had one of those roles you over-look if you weren't looking for her specifically. And that's what I was doing.

I sat in the back, I'm pretty sure she can't see me with the stage light on her face but I could see her every move.

"I knew that was you." Someone says standing in front of me, blocking my view.

"Wrong person, you're blocking me, move," I say to whoever it was, not in the mood to deal with anyone's bullshit today.

"That's how you treat your mentor now?" He says sitting next to me.

"What are you doing here Jason?" I say, irritation gone when I realized it was him but still keeping an annoyed face.

"Came to see a friend, you?"

"Same."

"Must be a lucky girl if you bought roses," He says pointing at the bouquet I was holding carefully, trying to make sure they don't touch my skin.

"Could say the same about you," I comment, pointing at the lilies in his hand.

"Touché," he laughs. "Which one is yours?"

"The prettiest one," I mumble, and quickly blush when I realize what I said.

"I hope we aren't here for the same girl buddy because I'm here for the prettiest one too." He teases, looking at the stage.

"I thought she was just a friend?"

"Could say the same to you," He bites back, using my previous word against me.

We stayed silent and watched the performance. My heart aches as I pray that we truly aren't here for the same girl.

Why do I care so much?

Because you like her dumbass.

Right. Shit.

"Let's go see if we're talking about the same girl," Jason says the moment the first part of the dance was over.

I nod and follow him as we make our way backstage. Thankfully there weren't a lot of people going back there so I didn't have to keep dodging people.

"That's my girl," Jason says pointing to where Aisha and another girl were standing. Please let the other girl be the one he's talking about. "Where's yours?"

I gesture to the same place and watch Jason's face pale, probably thinking the same thing as me. We walk towards the group, the tension high. The girls noticed us when we were close enough.

"Oh my gosh, what are you doing here?" Aisha says rushing

towards me and hugging me. I look at Jason giving the other girl the lilies and we both let out a sigh of relief.

"You're crushing the flowers," I whisper, giving her a smile behind my mask. She pulls back and takes them. I notice her eyes water a bit.

"Oh they're so beautiful," She mutters, taking them from my hand and putting them on a table. "Now hug."

I pull her into a hug. "I hope you don't mind me being here," I whisper and she shakes her head.

"Thank you for coming, it means a lot." She says.

"Wow, the first time I've seen him let someone touch him." Jason's voice pulls us out of our little bubble. "What's your secret?"

"Shut up," I say.

Aisha giggles and extends her hand. "Hi, my name is Aisha."

"Aisha, huh?" Jason says smugly, raising a brow at me, which goes unnoticed by Aisha.

"Everyone please finish what you're doing and make your way back to your seats." The announcement rang throughout the building.

"I'll see you after Sunshine," I tell Aisha, giving her a kiss on the forehead and going outside, Jason in a suit.

"Let's say it was a tie." He said once we sat down.

"No, I was right," I mutter, and he laughs.

Ten

AISHA

"Thanks again for coming," I tell Azrail, admiring the flowers he's given me. "It means a lot"

He hums out in response, a pink blush on his cheeks.

So cute.

"I understand why you're always late now," he mutters.

"What do you mean?"

"You're talented, it's obvious you put a lot of work into practice so it makes sense why you're late to class," He answers without breaking eye contact. "You're probably forced to leave for class."

I nod. He's not wrong, with my love of dancing and condition I never leave practice voluntarily. I'm never tired, sweaty, or sore.

"Are you sure you want to go to this party?"

Rosalie invited us to this party, it's supposedly a small get-together after the performance. Azrail and I got to her place 10 minutes ago, we stayed in my car to talk to each other. I wasn't going to go, but Azrail said yes so I decided to tag along.

"Jason won't stop bothering me if I don't and I'm pretty much covered so why not." He says, stepping out of the car and opening my door.

"I really hope it's as lowkey as she said," I mutter, remembering the parties I used to go to before everything happened.

He takes my hand in his and sends me a sweet smile. "Jason wouldn't make me go to a party that has too many people, don't worry."

"Does he know?"

"No, but he respects how I am without any questions."

"I like him," I giggle. "He's perfect for Rosalie."

"Just tell me when you're ready to go and we will, okay?" He says and I nod before ringing Rosalie's doorbell.

Seconds later the door swung open with a girl that looked similar to Rosalie smiling at us. Cindy, Rosalie's cousin, smile got ten times wider when her eyes landed on Azrail.

Not too much now.

"Hi, I'm Cindy." She says, extending her hand towards him, ignoring me.

"He doesn't like to be touched, where's Rosalie?" I speak, pushing her to the side and entering the house, Azrail in tow.

"Basement, you guys are the last one here." She says, walking into the kitchen, her eyes barely leaving Azrail.

"If I knew you were this protective, I would've befriended you a long time ago." He whispers hugging me from behind, I roll my eyes making my way downstairs with him in tow.

"What took you guys so long?" The first person who saw us, Jason, said smirking at us. I didn't have to turn around to know that Azrail was rolling his eyes.

"I'm gonna go say hi to the girls," I tell them and walk toward Rosalie and the girls she invited to the party. "I'm surprised you kept your word."

Rosalie rolls her eyes at my teasing, "Jason made me promise, saying that he and Azrail couldn't come if I wasn't true to my word."

"So you and Jason huh?"

"What about you and Azrail?"

We both blush at each other's teasing and decide to leave it be.

I'll admit, it's obvious to others that Azrail and I have something going on. It's natural for people to think we're dating, and not denying it allows us to keep the real secret.

I also admit that I started developing a tiny crush on him, but I doubt he feels the same way. For him, it's just an unspoken simple agreement

"You want something to drink?" Rosalie asks, pointing to the far table filled with drinks.

I shake my head. "I don't drink."

"Really, since when?" Cindy comments, slyly.

"What's that supposed to mean?" I question, raising a brow at her. She shrugs and walks away, a smug smile on her face.

"Ignore her, she just got broken up with." Anna, one of the girls, says giving me a sympathetic smile.

***

AZRAIL

"Either do that or skinny dip."

"Or I can just not do it, period."

"That's not how you play the game."

"I'll just skinny dip then," Aisha mutters.

"Why am I always part of a dare?" I ask Jason, taking another sip of my drink and enjoying the buzz.

The girls dared Aisha to come to kiss me or skinny dip. I

don't think they knew I could hear them, but besides Aisha, they're all drunk and giggling at the dare.

"Because you're Mr. untouchable," Jason jokes. "It's a party tradition at this point."

I roll my eyes at his comment. I walk towards the group, "What's going on?"

The girls start to giggle while Aisha sighs in frustration. She was about to speak up before someone spoke for her.

"She has a question for you?"

"What's up?" I ask, acting oblivious to everything.

"Yeah, can you watch my stuff while I go skinny dipping?" Aisha says and I roll my eyes at her stubbornness.

"You're not going into that water naked, you'll get sick," I tell her, crossing my arms and not leaving any room for discussion.

"I have to or…"

"Or…?" I ask, cocking a brow at her.

"I need to touch you." I hide my smile, acting as if I buy into her half-truth.

"Is that all?"

She gives a small shrug. I dip my face next to hers so we can make proper eye contact. "I'm not letting you into the pool so…"

"So….?" She whispers.

"Touch me, Sunshine, you're the only one who can," I tell her before pulling her into a kiss.

I don't know what I'm doing. I don't even know if I'm going to regret it in the future.

I blame the alcohol. I blame the alcohol. It's all because of the alcohol, nothing else.

But I know, that isn't true. I'm not even tipsy. I can blame the alcohol all I want. But deep down, I know. I know what everyone knows.

I'm infatuated with Aisha.

I want to consume her body and soul.
I want her, and will not stop until I get her.

Eleven

AZRAIL

As Aisha kisses me back only one thing stays in my mind.

I will worship her on earth and sing her name to the heavens. When I die and descend to hell and tell the devil of her, even he will get on his knees to worship.

He will understand how her beautiful soul can love the damned.

Her lips were soft, and I know I have none to compare them to but her kiss is the best.

"You know just a peck would be fine," Someone says, pulling me out of my fantasy as Aisha pulls away from me in a hurry. I glare at the girl who made the comment, as she glares at a flustered Aisha.

Jason smirks at me and I roll my eyes. Before any of us can say anything, Aisha's phone rings.

"Hi Daddy," She answers. Whatever her father said must've been good news by how much her eyes lit up. "I'm on my way."

She takes my hand and waves bye at the guest before dragging me out. "Sorry, my dad needs me I need to get home now. I hope you don't mind leaving early."

I shake my head and smile at her. I couldn't care less about leaving the party early, especially with that smile on her face.

"You don't have to drop me home, you know." I finally spoke but she shook her head and started driving at record speed. It scared me a little, but her excitement is so cute that I can't complain.

"Nonesense, we're almost here." She scoffs and makes a sharp turn, hitting the sidewalk. She sends me an apologetic smile and keeps driving.

We arrived at my house in five minutes, I live 15 minutes from her friend's house. It amazes and scares me how this woman managed to get me home safely.

"I'll call you okay," She says smiling at me and I nod. Leaving her car, a bit sad that she didn't mention the kiss. "Tell your mom I said hi."

"Get home safe," I tell her, not turning my back to face her.

"And Azrail," She yells out.

"Yes?"

"I'll call you soon. I don't regret anything from tonight," She winks, making me blush a little.

"Have fun with your dad sunshine."

With that last exchange, she left, driving a bit slower than previously.

❀ ❀

AISHA

"I'm home," I yell, rushing inside the house, happy to see what my father has planned for me.

"Slow down baby girl," He chuckles, coming out of the kitchen and hugging me. "Your surprise isn't going to run away."

From an outsider's point of view, they would be weirded out by my father's change of attitude but I'm used to it. We have our rough patches, that's true, but sometimes out of nowhere, he manages to surprise me.

"I know, I'm just happy to see you."

"Come on, your gifts are upstairs, get ready and we'll be going out." He says, giving me a warm smile, my mom laughs at my excitement as I run upstairs.

"Be careful," She says between laughs.

I open my door and as expected, a brand new wardrobe, a big bouquet of flowers, and some jewelry on the bed.

One thing about my dad is that gift-giving is his love language.

All the clothes and stuff he got me are things I have stared at for more than five seconds when we're out, or from my wishlist on different websites.

Two tickets caught my attention. I rush to it and scream out loud.

"I take it you like your gifts?" My dad says walking into my room and smiling. I nod vigorously.

"Thank you, Daddy," I rushed and gave him a hug.

"I figured we needed a father-daughter trip, " he says. "Put on the black dress I got you, we're going out to a company dinner."

"You must be Aisha, your father talks about you nonstop in the office." The white man says smiling up at me, he had salt and pepper hair and looked kind of like stan lee. His smile was warm and inviting.

"Good evening sir," I say, extending my hand for him to shake.

"Sir? You raise a good one, my children are never this behaved."

"Her mom deserves the praise, not me." My dad comments, giving me an approving smile.

He always feels pride when I go to his company events, people praise him for having a good family and that reputation makes his job more manageable. The easier his career is, the happier he is and the happier he is, the more he spends time with me.

"How was your performance, your dad could not stop talking about it nonstop." Mr. White asks.

"Really?" I couldn't hide my surprised expression, I never knew my dad talked about my dancing. I thought he hated it.

"Oh yeah, we can never get him to shut up, always talking about how much of a talented dancer his daughter is and how no one can stop you," Someone chimes in, a younger gentleman closer to my dad's age.

"That's enough Walter," My dad scowled, feeling a bit embarrassed at the sudden teasing.

My mom and I giggled at his reaction, making him more flustered. My dad hates letting people know he has a soft spot sometimes.

I give him a hug. He might've not shown up when I needed him, but he is definitely making up for it now.

My dad and mom stayed conversing with the coworkers while I slowly started getting bored.

As the night drags on, I remember the event from earlier, causing my cheeks to burn hot with fire.

I can't believe I kissed Azrail, scratch that, I can't believe he kissed me. His lips were soft, and they created a fire inside of me, something I'd never felt before.

He told me he was not experienced with these kinds of things, but somehow he knew exactly what he was doing and I almost didn't believe him.

"Do you want to stay here while your mother and I walk around?" My dad asks and I nod. I want to keep thinking about Azrail a bit more.

A few minutes went by before I decided to text him instead of overthinking our relationship.

ME

Hi Hi

TURTLE

Hey, what's up?

I stare in shock at how fast he messaged back.

ME

Nothing. I'm sitting bored at this company meeting.

TURTLE

Was that the surprise?

ME

No, just part of it. He got me gifts and tickets to congo, for our next father-daughter trip.

TURTLE

Is the trip an annual thing?

ME

Yeah, it used to be. Except for last year so I'm happy we're going again.

I've been dying to go to Congo so I'm glad that's where he picked for this year.

TURTLE

I'm happy for you.

> Why didn't you go last year?

> Where have you guys been so far?

> When do you leave?

> What other gifts did you get?

I smile at my phone, the first time I've had a guy keeping up the conversation. He makes it obvious that he does want to talk to me.

ME

Last year was a bad year.

We've been all over South America and some parts of Europe.

I leave for break, so I don't miss school.

I got a new wardrobe and jewelry

"Got a new boy toy already, I thought last year changed you." I rolled my eyes at the voice that interrupted me.

"Hello Jack," I mutter, rolling my eyes. "Don't you have a bitch to fuck?"

"I'm talking to her now,"

"In your dreams."

"Every night Princesa." He winks and I roll my eyes again, giving him a hug.

"I haven't seen you in forever, where have you been?"

"The old man sent me away to 'teach me a lesson' whatever that means." He says, rolling his eyes and making me laugh. "How are you though?"

"I'm good, just counting down to graduation."

"I forgot you were a little baby,"

"You are literally only two years older than me, relax on me."

"Yeah, I'm in my twenties, you're still a teenager." he points out.

"You're literally only twenty."

"Still older"

"Whatever," I say, rolling my eyes.

"Fine, I'll stop teasing," He says, giving me one of his sincere smiles. "Guess what?"

"What?"

"My old man and I are working on a case, and I'm going to be living here for a bit, you'll get to see me every day." He says clapping like a little child.

"Are you really in the case or are you just going to be filing papers?" I tease, and he rolls his eyes.

"It's a step up, I thought you would be happy for me. We can hang out more, or is your new boy toy more important than our friendship?" He fake pouts, I roll my eyes and hug him.

"Of course, I'm happy for you dummy, but it's my job to bully you."

"I love how you ignore my other comment, you like him don't you?"

"What's the case about?"

"It's confidential. Where did you meet him?"

"You can't tell your best friend?"

"Did you guys fuck already?" He asks, raising a brow. I roll my eyes, it's obvious that he isn't going to let it go.

"No, and we met at school. He's not a boy toy, he's a friend." I answer so he can leave me be.

"Just a friend?"

"Shut up," I grumble, hitting him and checking my phone to avoid his teasing.

TURTLE

I understand, whenever you want to talk about it. I'm here to talk. I can't wait for the little fashion show you're going to give with your new clothes.

ME

You know me so well :)

Twelve

AISHA

"How was your performance?"

"Good," I answered coldly, not in the mood to put up with Calvin. He's currently standing near my locker, insisting on us being all buddy-buddy like he did nothing wrong. "Don't you have someone else to follow around?"

"She's not here," He says, his eyes glossing over thinking about her. "Why don't you like her?"

"Who says I don't?"

"Alright, let's calm down," Jamila says, meditating between us. "We don't want to be late for lunch, it's wings Tuesday."

Calvin and I nod and follow her, wing Tuesdays are one of the best days. Unlike the other days, the food in the cafeteria looks edible.

I haven't seen Azrail since the party a few days ago and I miss him. We couldn't hang out this weekend because my parents had plans, and today is my first day back in school since last Thursday.

We talk on the phone often and it's been nice, there's no definition to our relationship, we just go with the flow.

"I feel like we haven't hung out together in so long," Jamila says. "I miss us, the trio."

"Yeah, life has just been so busy, we need to plan something," Calvin answers, sincerely.

"Just us three, like the old days." I finished.

Even though I only knew them for two months, I enjoy the bond I built with Calvin and Jamila. We fight like cats and dogs, but even so, I still consider them my best friends.

Maybe one day I will open up to them about my past.

"Why don't we do something for Halloween?" Calvin suggested.

"Can't, I got plans," I say.

Azrail and I are going to a carnival and a haunted house.

"With who?" Jamila asks teasingly.

"Azrail," I rolled my eyes at Calvin who already started opening his mouth to let out some bullshit. "If you know what's good for you, you will shut up."

"I do too, my parents aren't going to willingly let me go celebrate, so I'm going to my cousin and we're having our girl-only party," Jamila speaks up before Calvin and I get into another fight.

"We could have a Friendsgiving, just us three at my place, that would be fun." I pipe up. Friendsgiving has always been my favorite time of the year after my dance recitals.

"I'm down," Jamila muffles, enjoying her wings, and making us laugh.

"Bet, we got time to make sure everything is planned accordingly. No one is allowed to cancel, understood."

"Yes, ma'am," They say in unison.

"So, Azrail huh?" Jamila says, wiggling her brow.

"I gotta go," Calvin says, taking his stuff and walking out before we can say anything.

"Forget about him, spill," Jamila says, coming closer to me. "It's more than just friendship isn't it?"

"A little," I say, finally giving in. "We're just keeping it slow."

"Is that so?"

"Yeah, so don't do too much now."

"I won't, I won't," Jamila teases with her hand up in mock surrender. "He's perfect for you since you both like to keep your life private."

"Yeah right," I roll my eyes at her teasing. Before I could continue my thought, I noticed my pale boy walking into the cafeteria. "I'll be right back."

I watch him lean back on the wall, smiling at me as I make my way to him. He told me he was going to skip today, but I guess his mom told him otherwise.

"Hi," I whispered when I saw him. For some reason, whispering just felt right. I can feel Jamila's eyes burning holes on my back but I don't care.

"Good afternoon Sunshine," He whispers back. The tension between us is burning, embracing us in warmth. "Your friend is watching me like a hawk."

"I don't care, can I get a hug?"

The minute he nods, opening his arms and bringing me in. His scent gave me a sense of comfort and a warm feeling inside.

"I missed you too,"

"If you did, you wouldn't have tried to skip."

"It's not my fault, school is boring and you were gone for a while, did you miss me then?"

"Whatever," I roll my eyes and take his hand. "Do you mind sitting with Jamila and me for lunch?"

He looks at me for a bit before nodding. We walked to the

table Jamila was at, trying our best to ignore the not-so-subtle stares.

"I think it's funny how we've been in the same class for years, and it takes Aisha to make you sit near me huh?" Jamila teases, making me roll my eyes.

"Nice to formally meet you too Jamila," Azrail says quietly, squeezing my hand under the table. I smile at the interaction.

Jamila nods and turns her attention back to me. "So that new girl that Calvin has been hanging around, what do you think their deal is?"

"What'd you mean?" I try not to show my genuine emotions.

"One day he is fawning over her and wants us to hang out with her, and then the next he cancels at the last minute because "she's busy". I think she doesn't like us," Jamila says, popping a fry in her mouth.

"Well whatever it is, I don't care, it's between Calvin and her."

"Why don't you like her?" Jamila asks, knowing I'm hiding something.

"I have no ill feelings towards her, she just took my seat" I half lied.

"Mhm, sure." I roll my eyes, putting up a front and praying that Jamila doesn't continue.

"So..." Jamila spoke after a few minutes of silence. "When are you guys going to become official?"

Cue me choking on my drink, while Azrail turns into a tomato.

I shoot Jamila a glare.

"ATTENTION STUDENTS! FOR THE ASSEMBLY TODAY, MAKE SURE TO ATTEND YOUR LAST PERIOD AND WAIT FOR YOUR TEACHER TO DISMISS! I REPEAT, DO NOT SKIP YOUR LAST PERIOD YOUR TEACHER WILL DISMISS YOU."

"I forgot that this assembly was today," Jamila mumbles. "Do you know why we have a Halloween assembly now?'

Save by the principal.

I shake my head waiting for her to tell me the tea.

"A group of students did blackface and some dressed as the KKK for a haunted house, it created a riot. Authorities still don't know who did it, they say multiple high schools got in this together."

"What the actual fuck?"

"Yeah, now we have an assembly where they lecture us about culturally inappropriate outfits for Halloween and stuff. Last year was a mess."

"So you're telling me these students still walk these halls?"

"Well we aren't sure, some of them are said to have been seniors though. The investigation is still ongoing."

"I hope these fucking racists get what they deserve, what kind of fucked up shit is that." I start fuming, my voice getting louder. Azrail squeezes my hand, smiling sympathetically at me.

"I do too, it's 2026 and racism is still raining strong. It's tiring."

The bell rang before we could continue the conversation. I say bye to Jamila and walk to my locker with Azrail, too angry to care about the looks we were getting.

Azrail leans next to my locker while I angrily take my books out of my locker.

"I can't believe that people are still being this fucking stupid and still haven't gotten caught." I turn to face Azrail who gives me a small smile and pulls me into a hug. I breathe out, letting his peace consume me.

"Let it out," He whispers and pats my head. I breathe out and let a few tears drop.

"Come on, let me walk you to class." He mumbles after I calm down, taking my hand in his.

"Are you coming to the assembly?" I ask when we arrive in front of my class.

"If you save me a seat." He winks and kisses my forehead before I enter my classroom.

Thirteen

AISHA

My class is the last one to be dismissed, causing me to be mildly irritated because I already know it's going to be hard to find proper seats at the assembly.

The moment the teacher says we can leave, I was the first one to leave the class, stopping almost immediately when I saw Azrail staring at me.

"Why the rush?" He asks, grinning down at me.

"I want to get a good seat," I pout. "How'd you get permission to wait for me?"

"I don't have a last period." He says, holding my hand as we walk towards the gymnasium with the other students from my class in front of us.

"You don't have one or you chose not to go to one?"

He winks and says nothing. The gym was crowded and it seemed like there were no good seats saved, I turn to Azrail. Before I could say anything, I heard my name being screamed by a very loud Jamila.

She saved not one but two seats in the front for us. I could kiss her right now. Calvin was next to her glaring at Azrail, I turned to Azrail doing the same thing.

"We can find somewhere else if you want," I tell him, it also looks a bit crowded and I don't want him to feel too uncomfortable.

"It's cool, I'll be extra careful." He says and with that, we both walk toward Jamila and Calvin. I sit next to Jamila and Azrail next to me, creating a nice distance between the boys.

"Since when do you attend assemblies?" Calvin says to him.

"Since when did you care about my whereabouts Ben?" Azrail bites back.

The people around us acted like they weren't paying attention but it was obvious that they were. The testosterone between the two boys was choking up the room.

"Alright, settle down boys. The assembly is starting." I mediate between them, leaving no room for argument.

Calvin mumbles something under his breath but says nothing. I turn to Azrail and frown at him. He purposefully gets his name wrong, and I know Calvin is annoying but stooping to his level doesn't make it better.

"You don't attend assemblies?" I ask.

"Too many people," Azrail says, shrugging.

I paid closer attention to him, his left knee was shaking slightly and he was purposefully making himself small to not touch anyone. My heart breaks, he looks so vulnerable right now.

I bring myself closer to him, slightly nudging people around him to scoot a little further away. I got some looks but they moved with a quickness once they saw him.

"You didn't have to come, you know," I whispered to him.

"I wanted to," he says back, putting his hand on my knee and drawing circles. Something I notice he does when he is feeling nervous about something.

The assembly dragged on. First, the history teachers talked

about the history of Halloween for a brief moment, and then one of the counselors talked about what happened last year, how to be an ally and speak up, and the different types of resources to use if we get discriminated against.

Afterward, the vice principal did a slide show of what costume was deemed inappropriate and why. He included pictures of different mockery of races and the sexualization of religion. Following on how to do a costume without blackface and being racist overall.

I can't believe that this is something that still needs to be taught.

"Remember, if you have to think 'is this offensive' 9 times out of 10 it is." He finishes.

The teachers and students give a round of applause. After that, an all too familiar police officer and son duo come up to the stand making me perk up. I feel Azrail's eyes on me.

"We will now be finishing with one last announcement," The principal says.

I hear the students around us start to whisper, wondering if they caught the racists from last year.

"Good Afternoon Hoover High, my name is Officer Walker. This is my son, Jack Walker. We are both working on a case that we can't fully disclose but with Halloween coming up crime rate is rising and we would like for you guys to be safe." Officer Walker says, I raise a brow at Jack who caught my eyes and wink.

"There has been a series of murders," Officer Walker states, causing the students to go in upward. "Now calm down, you guys are not at risk. This killer is targeting drug dealers, and ex-criminals but some of the most recent ones have been within a 10-mile radius of this school. We ask you all to be careful, and if you have any suspicion or anything that could help us with this investigation please stop by the station and give a statement."

I look at Azrail who seems to be holding his breath, his leg shaking. I hold his hand and tighten my hold, trying to calm him down.

Could those murders be? No...

"My son Jack will be informing you guys how to be safe during the Halloween weekend."

I drown out Jack's voice and focus on Azrail.

"Breathe love," I tell him. Soothing him but it seems that it's not helping at all.

"What's wrong?" Jamila asks, raising a brow.

I shrug and take Azrail's hand. "We'll be back."

I dragged Azrail out carefully, going to an empty secluded hallway. He lets out a big breath and faints.

"AZRAIL."

Fourteen

AZRAIL

I don't know where I am.

It's dark, like a void.

I feel a presence, a presence that's both familiar and unfamiliar.

"Hello," I finally called out, my voice echoing through the void. "Where am I?"

"Asahi, you're all grown up."

I feel my heart writhed inside my chest at that name.

"Who are you? How do you know that name?" I call the stranger, putting my guard up even more.

"I gave you your gift, sweet child. Do you not remember me?" The voice, sounding sad, calls out softly.

"You mean the curse." I scoff. "Whoever you are, remove it. I don't want it."

"You asked for it. Why don't you want such a beautiful gift?"

"That gift is my punishment, isolated from the world, no one and nothing to turn to."

"Well, that's a lie. I put all these wonderful people in your path, your mom, your lover. I picked the best." The voice tries to justify.

"You expect me to thank you?" I seethed. "Mom's husband wouldn't have died if I never met him."

"Why are you looking in the dark side?" I didn't need to see the owner of the voice to know they were rolling their eyes. "What about that girl? She can touch and love you physically."

With that, my world shatters. It's because of them that Aisha can't feel, because of me, she has a short lifespan, and because of me she has a strain on her relationship with her father.

"You cursed her too? What do you want from me?" I cry out, eyes burning with tears.

"For the last time, it's not a curse, it's a blessing. I just want what's best for you, my sweet boy," The voice cooed, I felt a ghost touch on my cheek making me flinch.

"Azrail.................."

Aisha.

"Azrail.................Wake Up"

"Look I don't have much time, just remember you're blessed and you're not a killer." The voice says, their voice fading as Aisha's become louder.

"Who are you?"

"I love you my sweet boy," As the voice fades, and the room becomes brighter, I see a glimpse of a feminine figure walking away, her hair long and black, her figure slim and small.

"You're finally waking up." Aisha's voice, like a lullaby in my ears. I open my eyes, closing it quickly as the school light burns my eyes. I give it time to adjust before looking at Aisha.

She looked like a goddess looking down on me.

"How long have I been out?" I ask.

We were still in the hallway with my head on her lap.

"Two minutes," she mumms. Her eyes looked over me like I was a fragile thing.

"Really, it feels like forever," I mumble. Feeling at peace as she plays with my hair.

"What happened, Azrail?"

Moment over.

"Those murders," I start. "What if their all my fau-"

"Don't start, you're not a murderer." She cuts me off.

"Bu-"

"No,"

I get up from her lap and hold her shoulders. Staring into her eyes, that started to tear up.

"Aisha listen to me, I'm a ki-"

"What are you kids doing out here?" A voice comes out of nowhere, it's that police officer.

Aisha rolls her eyes and looks at him. "What do you want Jack?"

First name basis?

"You."

Excuse me.

"Can't you see I'm busy?"

"My bad princess, what's your name young man?" The officer says, extending his hand to me.

I say nothing, looking away. Trying to keep myself away from that cop.

"He's a germophobe." Aisha tells him, looking at me concerningly.

"Apparently mute too." That jerk mumbles and walks away when Aisha glares at him. Once he's out of view, I turn my attention back to Aisha.

"Old boyfriend?"

She rolls her eyes. "Don't mind him, he's just an annoying family friend. Are you feeling better?"

"Yeah, I think I just need to go home." I answer her, not in the mood to tell her about my dream yet.

"Come on, I'll take you."

＊ ＊ ＊

"Azrail, you've been in your room all day. Come eat." Mom says, knocking softly.

The ride home with Aisha was short and quiet. She stayed for a while but when she realized my mood, she left.

"I'm not hungry," I answer back.

A few seconds later, the door opens and I feel movement on my bed. Mom was sitting down carefully to give me one of her famous talks.

"Want to talk about what happened in school today?" She asks softly.

"Why ask? Aisha already told you."

"I want to hear it from you."

Realizing that she isn't going to give up, I sit up from my bed and face her. Her kind eyes send all the motherly love she can give me, without physically touching me.

"Some police officers came to school today, to give us a pep talk about Halloween and stuff," I start off, she nods. I appreciate that she was letting me start from the beginning even if Aisha already told her.

"Then they started talking about a series of murders that's been happening and I panicked," My heart starts to race, as I remember how I could be the reason all these murders keep on happening.

"Aisha managed to get me out of the gym and away from everyone, when I fainted." The closer I get to telling mom what happened, the tighter my throat gets.

"What happened during that? I feel like you're keeping something away from me."

"I heard this voice mom," I say quietly. "The voice said my real name."

Mom looks at me in shock. Even though she doesn't know my real name, because I refuse to say it out-loud. It took me years to even tell her that I was using a fake name, not that she didn't already know.

"What did the voice tell you?"

"The voice said my curse is a blessing," I say, telling her half the truth. I didn't have the courage to tell her that I'm probably the reason her soulmate is dead and Aisha is immune to pain. Just because this ghost wanted to put some good in my life.

"It is a blessing Azrail," Mom starts out. "You were being abused and your guardian angel sent something for you, it just has a couple of downsides, that's all."

"Always an optimist," I roll my eyes at her, too tired to fully fight back.

"And I wouldn't change it for the world." She answers back, winking at me.

"And Azrail, baby," She says, her voice is like how I imagined her hugs would feel. Warm, gentle, and caring. "You're not at fault for those murders."

"How do you know?" I ask, a tear dropping out of my eye.

"A mother always knows, and you are not a murderer Azrail." She says, I can see the pain in her heart when she realized she couldn't hug and comfort me.

"Thank you," I mutter, laying back down and facing away from her. It hurt too much to look her in the eye and not be able to hug her. I wipe away my own tears as always and wait for her to leave before breaking down into more sobs.

A few minutes passes and my phone vibrates.

SUNSHINE

How are you feeling?

Fifteen

AISHA

Azrail has been ignoring me for three weeks now. Well, not fully ignoring me, but as a girl that gets ignored by her father, I know what he's doing.

We meet up every Wednesday, Friday, and Saturday for our projects, and he will give me a goodbye and hello hug. He always makes sure I get home safe, but besides that, nothing. He even cancelled our Halloween plans, saying he had something to do.

He responds to my messages instead of having a conversation. He never teases or talks to me like he used to, no more cuddles, and he never brings up the kiss.

After the first week of his avoidance, I decided to also follow along and not bother him. After the second week, we don't text unless it's related to our project. I don't initiate hugs, and I start forcing myself to get rid of my crush.

It's obvious he doesn't want anything to do with me, so I might as well help him.

"What happened to your loverboy?" Jamila asks me, bringing

me out of deep thought. We were both at the nail salon getting our nails done, since Jamila just started her period she used it as an excuse for us to have a spa day.

"Who?"

"Azrail," she says like it was the most obvious thing in the world. "You guys used to be close and boom, distant. What happened?"

I shrug. Not saying anything.

"Aisha, I respect that you're reserved and want your own space but sometimes I feel like this friendship is one-sided, you listen to all my problems and help, but you never tell me anything."

"I'm sorry J, it's just, I'm not used to it." I admit feeling like a terrible friend.

"I know, and I know we've only been friends for a few months but I do appreciate our friendship and want us to grow."

We stay silent for the rest of the appointment as I contemplate on telling Jamila the truth.

"Azrail and I kissed," I said once we got in my car.

Jamila gasps, before letting out a squeal. "When??"

"The day of my performance," I say. "Everything was fine but then something happened in the assembly and he just became distant."

"What happened?"

I mentally scowl at myself, I said too much.

"The crowd made him panicky and I took him outside to calm him down, and Jack caught us when we were talking and bothered us a bit." I say, telling her half the truth.

"Jack?"

"The young police officer, he's two years older than us and an old friend."

Jamila bursts out laughing. I look at her in shock as she continues laughing to the point tears start to fall out of her eyes.

"You……are……special," She says between laughs, wiping her tears.

I look at her confused, "What?"

"It's clear that he's jealous."

"Jealous?"

"Yes, that police officer is pretty cute and probably acted very friendly towards you, so of course Azrail would get jealous."

"But I didn't flirt with him, I was focused on Azrail."

"Boys are dumb Aisha," Jamila says. "I think you should reach out to Azrail instead of ignoring him like you're ignoring Calvin."

"I'm not ignoring Calvin," I comment. "He stopped talking to me so I stopped talking to him, but when we see each other we're chill."

"Mhm, sure you are."

"What's that supposed to mean?"

"Come on, don't tell me you never noticed how Calvin looked at you,"

I stay silent.

"He had a crush on you, and I bet you his new little girlfriend Abigail noticed, that's why he's been distant with you and not me."

I cringe at that name. "But I never did anything, nor was I ever attracted to Calvin."

"You're an attractive woman, you don't need to do anything to be seen as a threat to these insecure girls."

I roll my eyes at that. I appreciate Calvin's friendship and all but he wasn't that important in my life for me to be depressed that we aren't close friends.

"Does that mean Friendsgiving is cancelled?"

"Not on my watch, we are still having it. I don't care if she gets mad," Jamila says, rolling her eyes and taking pictures of her new nails.

"So what are you going to do about Azrail?" She asks. I let out a sigh.

"Talk to him tomorrow I guess."

I have a feeling that his behavior is caused by something more than childish jealousy.

Sixteen

AZRAIL

I look at the beauty in front of me, blinking slowly as she stares down at me.

"What?" I ask slowly, not understanding her absurd question.

"I ask, do you hate me?" She repeats herself.

"Where the fuck did that idea come from?" I question. We were working on our project together, and out of nowhere, Aisha got up and stood in front of me, hands on her waist, looking pissed as fuck and asks me that fuckass question.

"Your behavior these past few weeks." She states, and I immediately feel guilty. She noticed.

"Oh."

"Oh? That's it," She closes her eyes and takes a deep breath. "Look, I'm used to men using and ignoring me all my life, so it really is no hard feelings. What I hate is when someone that clearly doesn't like being in my presence, forcing themselves to do so, like they pity me."

I pull her on my lap and hug her. "I don't hate you and I don't pity you."

"Then why Azrail, is it because of that kiss. Because if you don't feel that way, we can act like it never happened,"

I hold her tighter. "It's not because of that either."

"Is it Jack?"

"Who?'

"The police officer."

I roll my eyes and shake my head. "He makes me uncomfortable, but you didn't give him the time of day, so no."

"Then what is it Azrail?" She says pulling away from me and standing up.

I look down, too ashamed to meet her eyes.

"You know what, I think it's time for me to go." She says, before she could grab her things I pulled her back on my lap and kissed her.

It was a kiss of desperation and a longing. I miss having her next to me, miss the way it used to be, and if she leaves me after I tell her the truth might as well enjoy it one last time.

I finally pull away when I start to run out of breath. Our forehead touched, both of us panting and catching out breath.

"I had a vision," I finally spoke, not moving from our position. "The person in the vision talked about my powers and how it's a blessing."

After a minute of silence, Aisha speaks. "I'm sorry but how does that correlate with you ignoring me?"

I chuckled at that. "Sorry Sunshine, I was trying to figure out what to say next. The voice also told me that they put you and mom in my life to help me with this 'gift', which means if it wasn't for me, her husband would be alive and you probably wouldn't have had the illness that you have."

She scoffs at my words. I look at her in shock, this is not the reaction I expected.

"I don't know what happened to your mom's husband so I

can't speak on that but do you really think you're the cause of my illness?"

I nod.

"You didn't create me Azrail, and just because the voice said they put me in your path doesn't mean that they made me ill, there's different things that could've happened that made it possible for us to meet."

"Bu-"

"But nothing Azrail, this illness that I have, is something that runs in both sides of my family, some just happened to be lucky to not get it. It's not your fault that I happened to have it, the risks were very high and my parents chose to go through the pregnancy."

"I'm sorry," I said.

"For what?"

"For being a coward and not speaking to you, for making you feel insecure about us instead of communicating."

She hugs me and laughs. "It's okay love, it must not have been easy."

"Aisha?"

"Hm?"

"What did you mean by your use to men using you?" I finally ask, her body stiffening at that question.

"It's just that, I was always the girl that got kissed, asked for nudes, and stuff, never the one that got asked out and became a girlfriend," She admits. That confession angered me, how dare they just use her like that. "So I thought it was the same with you."

I grab both of her cheeks and stare into her eyes. "Listen to me Sunshine, I will never do that to you. You're mine, and I'm not letting you go."

"If you say so," she says giggling a little and laying on me.

"Aw you guys are so cute."

"Mooommmm," I groaned, feeling embarrassed while she and Aisha laughed.

❀ ❀ ❀

"I need your help."

"You're asking me for help? This is new,"

I roll my eyes, "Will you help me or not Jason."

"With what exactly?"

"…To plan a date," I whisper.

"What was that? I didn't quite hear you, for a second there I thought you were asking me to help you plan a date."

"Can you please be serious?"

"Holy shit dude, you finally asked out Aisha?"

I nod. After clearing up the misunderstanding, I asked her on a date last night. I didn't want her to think I was just using her. The thing is, I never dated so I don't know what to do.

"Okay okay, when is the date?"

"Saturday,"

"What do you have planned?"

"I wouldn't be asking you for help if I had something planned."

"Keep up that attitude and you won't be getting any help,"

"Sorry."

"It's cool, you're just nervous, let's brainstorm." Jason says chuckling. "You're a student, meaning you're not rich enough to go to a high end restaurant with her, so let's think of something simple."

"Okay."

"The movies?"

"Too many people,"

"Skating?"

"Too many people,"

"Amusement park,"

"Too many pe-"

"Don't even finish that," Jason says, rolling his eyes. "What do you guys do when you usually hang out?"

"Cuddle."

"That's so cute it's disgusting," he teases. "What is Aisha like?"

"She loves hugs, dancing and snacks. She's a hopeless romantic, caring, and guards her heart. She loves hallmark movies, and anything cheesy, sh-"

"Okay Romeo, I get it," Jason cuts me off. "You are whipped, but it's a good thing because I know exactly what kind of date you two should have."

"What?"

"A cliché date, duh." A voice says, I turn around and see Rosalie at the door smiling at us.

"I called her," Jason says, pulling her on his lap.

I roll my eyes.

"Please don't make me regret asking you."

Seventeen

AISHA

"Did he tell you where you guys are going?" Jamila asked.

"No, he just said to dress cute and casual," I responded. "What do you think?"

I show Jamila my favorite yellow sundress with frills on the bottom.

"I love, what time is he getting here?"

"In 10 minutes, why am I so nervous?" I say, pacing around my room, feeling a sense of panic overwhelming me.

"It's your first date. Of course you're nervous." Jamila says, smiling at me.

Before I could say anything back, my doorbell rang. "I guess it's time to go, bye J."

"Stay safe and keep me updated, love." She says, we blow air kisses to each other before I hang up the phone and rush downstairs.

"I thought we told you not to run down the stairs?" He says, giving me a playful scowl.

"Who said I ran down?"

He raises a brow and I sigh in defeat. "Fine, I'm sorry it won't happen again."

He gives me a kiss on the forehead and holds my hand. I follow him out, feeling a bit shy since it is her first date ever.

"How was your appointment?" He asks as we start walking out to a car I've never seen before.

"Good, no injuries, just a few cuts and bruises but that's normal since we've been getting more intense at practice." I answer, as he opens the passenger door for me.

"Azrail?"

"Yes Sunshine?" He says

"Whose car is this? And why are you driving?"

"Jason helped me get my drivers license, mom bought me this car a long time ago I just couldn't drive it legally." He answers winking at me.

"You got your license and didn't tell me," I pout, hitting his shoulder slightly.

"Yes Sunshine, I wanted it to be a surprise."

"So where are we going?"

"It's a secret, here," he says, handing me the aux-cord which I happily oblige and put some music on.

"I love your hair today, the puffs are cute." He comments, his cheeks tainting red, mine also heating up at his compliment.

"Thank you, I wanted to try something new, I'm thinking about dying it."

"What color? So we can match."

"Really?" I squeal. That would be so cute, but would that be moving too fast.

"Well not my whole hair, but I would get highlights that color."

"I'll definitely hold you up to that." I say, cheesing.

"Wow," I whisper, looking at the sight in front of me.

The drive to this location took about an hour. On our way there Azrail got me my favorite snacks and we spent the whole car ride talking and just enjoying each other's company. It was nice.

I'm currently looking at a nicely decorated backyard with a treehouse. The trees had fairy lights on them, but they weren't turned on because it was still light out. The backyard led to a forest, and there was a small pond surrounded by flowers and decorative stones.

"You like?" Azrail asks, giving me a back hug as I enjoy the scenery.

"Yes, but whose house is this?"

"Mines."

"Yours?"

"Yes, after mom's husband died she decided to keep one of his properties and gave it to me as a gift on my 16th birthday," He explains. "She wanted me to have a place where I can just go when I want to and since I'm still young, I list it on renting sites so I can make some money."

"Wow," I say again. "That is true entrepreneurship right fucking there, is that what you want to do?"

"Being in real estate has been tempting, but it requires some socializing that I can't do." He says, sounding sad.

I give him a big hug, "Let's see what's up in that treehouse."

He smiles down at me and guides me to the treehouse, helping me climb it.

"Oh wow," I say for what feels like the fiftieth time tonight when I saw inside the treehouse.

The floor of the treehouse was covered with blankets and

there was a big panda bear in the corner. There was a small table with snacks, pillows everywhere and a projector.

I jump on the big teddy bear.

"Be careful," I hear Azrail say but I ignore his warning and give him a big hug. "Thank you turtle, I love it."

"Turtle?" He asks, raising a brow.

Right, I never called him that out loud.

"Yes, that's been your name on my phone."

"I like it, it's unique." He says, making me smile even more. "I know it's not Christmas yet, but I was thinking a Hallmark movie?"

"You know me so well," I coo, adjusting myself so that he has a spot next to me while I also get to cuddle with the panda.

"Don't tell me this panda is going to replace me,"

"Um I don't know, he is pretty big and cuddly."

He pulls me close to him, the sudden movement makes me squeal. He leans and whispers in my ear, "I'm better Sunshine."

"You're really going to get jealous of a bear that you gave me?" I teased him but didn't pull away from his embrace.

"Yes, and?"

"You're something else." I laughed before focusing on the movie that was starting.

After the movie ended, the sun was starting to set. Azrail and I enjoyed each other's company. It was a beautiful sight.

As the sun sets, the fairy lights turned on. We stayed under the moonlight, talking about our hopes and dreams.

"Aisha,"

"Hm," I hum back, eyes close as I feel sleep slowly start to take over me.

"I know this is our first date and all," Azrail starts. His heartbeat increased. "But,but I was wondering if I could be your boyfriend?"

"Of course turtle," I snuggle closer to him and peck his lips before laying on his chest. I blame my sleepy state for my calm reaction,

Best first date ever.

Eighteen

AISHA

"I don't like that, Clark," Azrail scoffs and I roll my eyes.

"I know you don't like Calvin, but we planned this Friendsgiving thing a long time ago," I told him. "I would invite you but we made a promise that it would be just us three."

"I don't mind Sunshine, but he's just a bad friend," He says. "He ignores you all the time now and only focuses on that girl."

"Yeah but J wants this too, I'm mainly doing it for her."

"Fine, I like her, just don't hug him."

"I won't," I say, raising my hand up in surrender. "I'll keep you updated and will stay far away from him, pinky promise."

Before he could say anything my doorbell rings. I start to rush downstairs but stop when Azrail yells at me.

"Sorry turtle," I laugh.

I open the door and my smile immediately drops. Jamila, Calvin and *Abigail* are at the door.

"Um, hi." I said confusingly, raising a brow at Clark. I thought we had agreed it was just going to be the trio.

"Hey, Abbey's going to join us, I forgot to tell you." He says sheepishly. Jamila looks irritated while Abigail has a smirk on her face.

"Don't get mad at him, I insisted, I felt too anxious letting him hang out with you girls alone," She says, snaking her hands around his arm and kissing him. "You should know what I mean."

Jamila looks at me questionably, silently asking me what was wrong. I suck up the sunken feeling in my stomach and give a fake smile, inviting them in.

"Oh wow, you went all out this year." Abigail commented, I roll my eyes.

"Love the decorations Aisha," Jamila said, walking around and putting her food on the table.

"Is everything okay?" I hear Azrail's voice in my ears. I forgot I was on the phone with him.

"Yeah, um, everyone is here so I'll be going now." I mumble, ignoring the knot in my stomach.

"Do you need me to come? I heard what Clark said." He says, I shake my head, sending him an air kiss before hanging up.

I walk in the kitchen, putting on my best fake smile.

"Were you on the phone with your boo?" Jamila teases trying to ease the tension in the room, I roll my eyes at her.

"Yeah,"

"You're in a relationship?" Calvin asks, looking pretty shocked. I roll my eyes and just nod.

"They've been together for almost a month now, you would know if you hung out with us more." Jamila sneaks diss and I walk away to take the food out of the oven, not wanting any part in this argument.

"Congrats," Abigail says and it takes my all to not run out of the house. *Why the hell does she have to be here?*

All the food was now on the table and we were ready to feast. There was small talk between Jamila, Calvin and Abigail while I stayed quiet making my own plate. Jamila tried to bring me in the conversations but I kept it short, clearly feeling uncomfortable.

"So Aisha, Abbey told me tha-" Before Calvin could finish what he was about to say the bell rings.

"Did you invite anyone else? I thought it was going to be just you three?" Abigail spoke, I ignored her and went to the door.

What was Calvin about to say? Did she tell him already?

I opened the door and was instantly pulled into a hug.

"What are you doing here?" I asked the short latina that was still hugging me.

"I invited her,"

"And what are you doing here?" I ask the white man behind her.

"I invited him," I smiled at the Japanese boy behind him. *My Japanese boy.*

"And what are you doing here?" I ask, a small smirk on my face as I went to hug him.

"You really think I was going to let you be with her all day." He whispers in my ear.

"Thank you" I whisper back, he hums in response.

"I hope you don't mind. I also brought another friend, he's getting the games out the car," Jason says and I nod. "I'll go get the drinks."

"Who was it?" I hear Jamila yell from the other room.

"Some friends who decided to crash," I say smiling and walk in the room with Rosalie and Azrail in tow. Soon after Jason and his friend also came into the room, Jason with drinks and his friend with some board games.

"This is my friends, Rosalie, Jason, you already know Azrail, and I'm sorry I didn't catch your name." I said to Jason's friend as I was introducing everyone.

"Saad," He was a brown man with a deep. I couldn't help but notice Jamila looking down, blushing.

Something to tease her about later.

"Yes, nice to meet you." I smile. "And this is my best friend Jamila, Calvin and his girlfriend."

"Since the trio rule got broken, I hope you guys don't mind the extra company." Azrail says, holding my hand and glaring at Calvin. It takes my all to not smile at his pettiness.

The group introduces themselves with each other, Saad sat next to Jamila and introduced himself to her, she had a slight pink taint on her cheek. We all sat down and ate, the environment was lively and surprisingly nice. Azrail didn't talk but it was fine, he was holding my hand under the table and was constantly putting food he didn't like on my plate.

"So how do you guys know each other?" Abigail asks, bringing back the uneasy feeling.

"Azrail here has been coming to my shop since he turned sixteen," Jason spoke, extinguishing all tensions. "He was a weird kid, wanted tattoos but wanted to do them himself so I took him under my wings and taught him."

"So Aisha is the only person allowed to touch you?" Jamila asks, wiggling her brows at us.

Azrail nods, a small blush on his cheek.

"Rosa came to my tattoo parlor and we started talking and I went to her dance recital and the rest is history," Jason says, kissing her hand. "And this teddy bear over there has been my best friend since kindergarten, we grew up next to each other."

Saad rolls his eyes. "He wouldn't leave me alone so I'm stuck with him."

"Oh Saad baby, you know you love me."

"So, Ben's girlfriend, how did you get so comfortable in this group that you just invited yourself at their friendsgiving hang-out." Jason says bluntly, earning a gasp from me and a soft hit on the shoulder by Rosalie.

Before I could apologize for his bluntness, Abigail spoke. "Who's Ben?"

"Calvin, my name is Calvin,"

"Oh," Jason says. "Azrail told me Ben, my bad bro."

"Our teacher put us next to each other and Calvin was so chivalrous and nice, helping me catch us with school that I just fell for his charm."

I look at Jamila who makes the same face as I.

What charms?

"But," Abigail says looking at me, giving me one of her fake smiles. "Aisha and I go way back, we went to the same school before she transferred."

Chatter broke out when she announced that. "You guys were friends?" Jamila asks, surprised with the new information.

Before I could say anything, she spoke. "We weren't friends or anything, I was also in the background and she was miss popular so she probably doesn't remember me."

I give a tightlipped smile while everyone looks at us in shock. Except for Calvin, it's obvious he already knew.

How much does he know? What is her gameplan?

"Aisha? miss popular? She hates getting attention." Jamila spoke, clearly confused with this new fake.

"Yeah, she was in all clubs, and even was a cheerleader, she won junior princess, and everyone already knew she was going to be Prom Queen before she left."

Please, shut up.

All eyes were on me and before I could say anything we heard a big pop scaring all of us.

"Oops," Jason says, holding a bottle of champagne, dripping on the floor. "I could never open those properly."

"I'll get paper towels," I say getting up.

"Thank you," Jason says, giving me a subtle wink as I walk

away. I don't even have to turn around to know that Azrail was following me.

"How are you feeling?" He hugged me tightly. I felt a tear drop out of my eye and I let it go.

"I'm tired." I mutter.

"Let's take a walk," He says, taking the paper towel and mop. Jason walks in the kitchen before we can leave.

"Here," Azrail tells him. "Aisha and I are going for a walk."

Jason nods understandingly and leaves the room without saying a word. Azrail and I walk out, my head down so no one can see I was crying.

"We'll be back soon, Jamila, you're in charge." Azrail says, grabbing our coats.

"Why am I not in charge?" Jason yells.

"She's more responsible." Azrail yells back and he scoffs, while I let out a small laugh at their bickering.

After putting on our coats, Azrail opens the door for me and we're out. We walk for a bit, hand in hand and in silence. After a while he pulls out a blunt, lighting it and passing it to me.

"Ah so it's one of those walks." I giggle, inhaling and passing it to him.

"I felt like you needed it." I nod. He's right.

"I guess you want an explanation,"

"You don't have to." He says understandingly.

"No, I want to." I say, taking a big inhale before I say anything.

Well, here goes nothing.

"Abigail was my best friend and I slept with her boyfriend."

Nineteen

AZRAIL

I blink at this new piece of information. Surely there must be some kind of reason, my Sunshine would never.

"I know you're already disgusted by me, I won't be surprised if you don't want to date me anymore." She says, her eyes already tearing up.

So it is true.

I shake my head and wipe her tears away. "You're not getting rid of me that easily,"

"Yeah, wait till you hear the rest." She scoffs, not believing me.

I look at her, waiting for her to continue.

"You already know I have a mountain load of parental issues, especially when it comes to getting affection from my father." She starts, I nod.

"Well, I started acting up to get his affection. I started going out and coming home drunk, and I will go missing for days, but that did nothing."

That's why she doesn't drink anymore.

"I still did decent in school but I did everything for attention, from sleeping around and even having a reputation."

Oh.

"Sleeping with guys made me feel the warmth that my dad never gave me, and alcohol allowed me to 'feel' even though it was all in my head, if that makes sense. The only healthy thing I did was ballet and collecting stuffed animals."

She stops, taking another inhale, her eyes are starting to turn red.

"Abigail was the nice girl everyone loved, a quiet little nerd and we just became friends. We confided in each other and it was a judgment freezone." She says, reminiscing.

"She started dating this guy, but refused to tell me who it was because he wanted to keep it a secret. One day, we got invited to this party and she didn't want to go and we got into a fight because I didn't want to go alone."

"I eventually left and went to the party and had my fun. This boy, in the football team, came to me and offered me a drink and I took it. I remembered Abigail had a crush on him but the moment she got into a relationship, she stopped talking to him. He wasn't my type at all, but the drink he gave me made me feel warm and dizzy so he took me to a room."

"Next thing I know, I woke up, no clothes on me and my phone ringing. I'm used to blacking out but never like that so I already knew there was something wrong. I answered my phone and it was both of my parents yelling and telling me to come home, I was late for my checkup."

"I went home and they took me to the hospital," She started sobbing by then and I hugged her, a part of me already knew where this was going and it broke my heart. "The doctor, um the doctor came and said that it seemed that I've been rape and need stitches."

"My parents didn't believe in the rape because they knew my

history but when they saw that I couldn't remember what happened, they believed me immediately and called the police. The damage was already done, the moment I looked at my phone I got spam messages of Abigail cursing me out and sending me a video of me and her boyfriend kissing me. She said I was the worst friend and that she will make my life a living hell."

She breaks down into sobs, I comfort her. "It's not your fault Sunshine, breathe."

"She had someone post all my nudes on social media, and since she was loved by all, everyone in school hated me for sleeping with her boyfriend. My parents got Officer Walker, Jack's father, on the case but with my reputation he only got expelled and the person who leaked my nudes got probation for child pornography. Abigail did not receive any punishment, I even got suspended for taking those pictures."

"I started getting bullied and harassed everywhere I went, so my parents decided to pull me out of school, homeschool me the rest of junior year and transfer me here for my senior year. They act like they aren't mad or disappointed in me, but I know the truth, it took months for my father to look me in the eye."

We stay quiet. Aisha keeps smoking the blunt, not saying anything to me or even looking at me.

"Aisha,"

"Hm,"

"Look at me Sunshine," I say softly and wait for her to do so. "You did not sleep with your best friends boyfriend, you got raped by a guy you didn't even know she was seeing and she is a horrible friend for doing all of those things to you."

"You're not disgusted by me? My past?"

"Aisha, I've killed people, we all have a past we aren't proud of," I say, I smile when I notice her lip twitching at my comment. "I can never be disgusted by you, you're my Sunshine."

I pull her into a hug.

"Turtle,"

"Yeah?"

"It's too early to say I love you but I do want to say, I really do appreciate you."

"I appreciate you too Sunshine, more than you could ever know."

🐢　🐢

"I bet that walk was nice, you two look fried as fuck." Jason teases when Aisha and I walk in the house, everyone was in the living room, Charlie Brown was on the TV and they all seem to have been drinking and playing board games.

Saad and Jamila sat next to each other, talking about something in Urdu. Rosalie had Jason laying on her lap, and Ben and Abigail looking our way not saying anything.

"Shut up Jason,"

"Is this how you treat your best friend," Jason asks, clutching his chest, fake hurt. I roll my eyes and sit in the corner of the couch, Aisha sitting next to me smiling at us.

Her friends Jamila and Rosalie give her an *'are you okay?'* look and she smiles.

"So when is you guys' end of the year performance?" Jamila asks the girls.

"December 24th," Rosalie answers.

"Sorry I won't be able come," Ben speaks, Jason rolls his eyes,

"It's cool," Aisha says giggling because she saw Jason's eye roll.

"You already know Azrail and I will be there cheering for you girls, front row seats and everything." Jason says, wiggling her brow at Aisha who was now laughing uncontrollably, making us laugh also.

She was such a happy person when high.

"Aisha, you leave the 27th right?"

"Yeah, and I'll be back on January 4th," She answers in between laughs. My heart aches at that.

"Aww Azrail is sad," Rosalie squeals, making everyone look at me. I roll my eyes at her and put on my earbuds to ignore her. Unlike Aisha, I preferred total silence and isolation when high.

That didn't last long before Aisha took out one earbud to whisper in my ear, "I'll be back before you know it turtle,"

"You guys are adorable," Saad finally spoke, everyone nodded in agreement.

Well not *everyone*.

I look at the couple that was further away from us, Ben clenching his jaw and Abigail looking out of place.

I bet she regrets coming now.

"Well, this is way more than just 'three people'". A voice says, interrupting us. We all turn and look at the owner of the voice in shock.

"Oh shit," I hear Jason whisper, followed by a smack from Rosalie.

We're in trouble.

"Ma, Daddy," Aisha says, jumping off the couch and running towards her parents.

"No running," Her parents, Jamila, Calvin, and I say in unison. I feel myself getting red when they raise a brow at me, Aisha laughs at that and hugs her parents.

"I thought you guys were coming back tomorrow?" She says to her parents.

"We decided to crash early, are you going to introduce us?"

Aisha turns around and starts to point at all of us. "This is my boyfriend Azrail, my ballerina partner Rosalie, the one I've told you about, Azrail's friends Jason, Jason's friend Saad, and you already know the rest."

"Yes, hello Abigal." Aisha's father says, glaring at the girl who gulps in return.

"Hi s-sir."

"Aisha," Her mom starts, but decides against it. "Whatever. Everybody, relax we aren't mad, we prefer everyone to be safe under our roof than outside, continue having fun, we'll be retreating into our room."

Everyone lets out a breath of relief while Aisha laughs, expecting that reaction.

"Baby, get that girl out of my house, it's ruining my energy." Aisha mom tells her, in a not so subtle whisper. I smile at that.

Aisha nods, giving both her parents a hug goodbye. Her mom retreats upstairs first, while her father waits for a bit.

"Will we get the chance to properly meet your *boyfriend* soon?" He says to Aisha and she nods.

Well shit.

Twenty

AISHA

"I'm starting to regret this," I mumble. Ever since I introduced Azrail as my boyfriend to my parents they've been insisting on meeting him, and I suggested inviting him to our thanksgiving dinner.

The worst fucking thing I ever said.

I forgot that my extended family was coming too. There's not a lot of us in the state, but it's still too much. My cousins, grandparents, aunts and uncles. There will be a total of twenty-five guests, not including me, my parents, Azrail, and his mother.

"We don't need to come, I can just tell my mom I don't want to go." He says, looking at me with concern in his eyes.

I shake my head. No, I invited them and I wanted them to meet my parents. This is going to happen.

"Will you be comfortable? There will be a lot of people." I say. Even though I told my parents and family that he is a germa-phobe, you can never be too sure.

"I'll be fine Sunshine, I know you have my back." he says smiling.

I sigh and walk up to him, fixing his tie. My family came to the house last night and I needed a break so I went to his house and decided to get ready with him and his mother.

"Do your parents hate me?" He asks softly.

"Why would you say that?"

"I don't know, some people think I'm pretty stuck up for not wanting to touch them."

"It's fine Azrail, one thing about my parents is they're understanding, they won't judge you for that."

"Are you sure?"

"Yes, I am." I say giving him a peck on the lips.

Just then his mom starts walking down the stairs, looking beautiful as fuck.

"Oh wow, you look gorgeous ma'am" I say. She has a formal brown dress that shows all her curves, not that she could ever hide it. "When I get older, I'm definitely locking my hair."

She has beautiful silver locks that reach her waist. It's obvious she had them for years and it fits her beautifully.

"Thank you love," She says, giving me a hug. "Are you guys ready to go?"

Azrail and I nod, grabbing our coats. Since my mom dropped me off at Azrail's house, we were all going in Azrail's mom's car. Azrail and I sat in the back, both of us obviously nervous for tonight, while Azrail's mom was just rapping to Tupac.

My mom already briefly met Azrail's mom and Azrail from that time I was in the hospital so I'm not worried about them meeting at all. It's just my dad and other family I'm worried about. My cousins are going to embarrass me and tease Azrail and my dad, I don't know how he will be. Which makes it worse.

He's been home more often, making me spend less time with Azrail. I came home late on Monday and he asked me fifty million questions when I told him I was with Azrail, now I get home before the sunsets.

The car ride was short since we didn't live too far from each other. Azrail opened my door for me and we made our way to the house, music and chatter could be heard already.

I unlock the front door and step in with my guest. Azrail touched my hand, assuring me everything will be alright.

"We're here." I yell out. At the sound of my voice, footsteps run towards my direction.

My cousins.

"So this is the famous boyfriend?"

"He's taller than I expected,"

"I see you cuz, he's not ugly,"

"Who's the fine lady next to him?"

"Happy I finally get to see his face and not that soft launch shit Aisha does in her social media."

My dad comes in the hallway and clears his throat, quieting everyone. I send him a thankful smile.

"Everyone, this is Azrail and his mother."

"Oh shit, that pale boy is mixed?" My eldest cousin says, and I roll my eyes at him.

"I'm adopted." Azrail answers.

"That's cool, this dipshit is adopted." He says pointing at his younger sister, earning a smack from my aunt.

"Stop telling everyone your sister is adopted." She scowls and I mentally thank her.

We're off to a good start.

"Everyone please go back to the living room, and allow our guests to get settled before you start bombarding them with questions." My dad says ushering my aunt and cousins out.

"Sorry about that," I apologize quietly, Azrail and his mom shake their heads with a smile.

"Quite a lively family." His mom commented and I feel my cheeks get warm.

"Relax Sunshine, there's nothing wrong with that, we're just not used to it." Azrail says, kissing my forehead.

We took off our coats and walked to the living room where everyone was. My mom went and hugged Azrail's mom. Their relationship grew closer with all of my visits to the hospital, now they're close to becoming best friends.

"So glad you could join us," My mom says, letting go of the hug and smiling at Azrail.

Azrail bows at her and my family, "Thank you for inviting us."

"No need, you're basically family now dating my daughter."

"When we heard that Aisha got a boyfriend we didn't believe it, guess you are real." My uncle says laughing.

"We thought those only existed in books for her," My aunt joins in, now everyone is laughing, even Azrail had a small smile on his face.

I rolled my eyes, but also smiled. I love when they come, they light up this big house.

"Dinner's ready," My dad says walking out of the kitchen and we nod following. Azrail and I sat towards the end, to make sure no one sat next to him. His mother was next to me, my parents sat in front of us and my other family were scattered around.

"So how long have you guys been dating?" My dad asks, looking at Azrail.

"Since November 7th," Azrail answers.

"And since when were you interested in Aisha?" One of my cousins asked.

Since when did this become an interview?

"Since August."

A small cough leaves me and I turn around looking at Azrail in shock. He doesn't look at me, a small smirk on his lips.

"I guess Aisha wasn't aware of that," one of my cousins says.

Everyone laughs at that comment while I'm still looking at Azrail in shock.

"How much do you know about Aisha?" My dad asks, there is slight tension because my family knew exactly what he meant.

"The past, the present, and not to sound like a wizard, the future." Azrail says with a smile, kissing my forehead.

Oh, he's killing it.

My dad nods, giving him a smile. The official seal of approval.

"So her illness doesn't bother you?" My younger cousin asked.

"Nope."

"Even if she's destined to die early."

Where's the kids table when it's needed?

"She's not destined to die early idiot, she just needs to be more careful, greatgramgram lived till 98 and she was sick too," My other cousin says, rolling her eyes at her sibling. "Are you sure this one isn't adopted?"

"And with modern technology, there's definitely nothing to worry about." Azrail mom says when the tension in the room didn't go down.

Azrail grabs my hand, his leg bouncing.

He's anxious.

"So what colleges are you kids going to next year?" My aunt, Carol, says earning a grown from us three seniors.

That's a way to change the subject. Azrail and I shrug, I don't even think he's going to college and I'm not sure what I really want to do. I know dancing is going to be my focus, but I'm not sure about my backup plans.

"We applied to numerous schools, so we'll see what we're going to choose when we get accepted." I answer for us.

"Well whatever you choose, make sure it's you." My mom says.

"You don't want to follow your dad's footsteps anymore?" Uncle Jerome asks.

I shrug.

He barely has time for family because of that job, I'm not sure I want that anymore.

"She's growing up, that's how they are." My dad says light-heartedly. I ignore the slight sting in my heart and also smile.

"What are your interests son?" Dad asks Azrail.

Son?

"I'm thinking about real estate."

"I work in real estate, have Aisha give you my information and we can work something out when you graduate." Aunt Carol says.

Oh, I forgot about that.

"Thank you ma'am."

The rest of the dinner went smoothly, Azrail and his mom were treated like family and it was no longer awkward between us.

I gave my yearly dance for my family, because the grownups always offered me money for me to do my little dance, since I was a child.

The day was ending and Azrail and his mom said their good-byes and I walked them out. Azrail mom gives me a hug.

"Thank you for this Aisha," She says. "My husband and I are estranged from our family so it's always been Azrail and I for the holiday, this has been a nice change."

"No need to thank me ma'am, you guys are invited anytime."

She pulls away and goes to her car, leaving me and Azrail. He pulls me into a deep kiss, fireworks exploding in my stomach.

"Thank you, Sunshine."

Twenty-One

AISHA

"Alright class, we have 24 days left before the performance," Coach says to us as we prepare for one last run-through.

Everyone in the class looked exhausted and ready to pass out. This is one of the days where I'm happy that I can't relate.

For the end-of-the-year performance, we're doing *The Nutcracker*, and I'm the Sugar Plum Fairy. I originally wanted to be Clara, but the Sugar Plum Fairy's part is the hardest, and I can do it effortlessly without being tired, so I tried out for that part.

Once we finish our last run-through and are stretching before leaving practice, Rosalie comes next to me with a big smile on her face.

"What's the good news?"

"Jason proposed."

"He WHAT!?" I send an apologetic smile to my coach and teammate for disturbing them.

"Yeah."

"And what did you say?"

"Yes."

"You WHAT!?"

"Aisha, I'm 22, he's 24—there's nothing weird about that. We aren't teenagers," she says, giggling at my reaction.

"Yeah, I know. It's just that… you guys just met."

"I know, but when you know, you know. And we aren't even going to start planning the wedding until I finish with my master's, so don't worry."

"Does that mean kids in the future?"

"Not until I'm closer to 28."

"Congratulations," I finally told her, giving her a big hug. "I can't wait for when I get proposed to—in the far, far future."

Rosalie laughs at my comment. "The way Azrail looks at you, I doubt it will be that far in the future."

"What do you mean?"

"At your Friendsgiving, he was focused on just you," she gushes. "And the way he came to Jason's place and demanded that we come to your house because you have a 'bitch-ass friend'—his words, not mine."

Wow, he really did that for me.

I feel my cheeks flush thinking about Azrail's actions.

"You know, I've always wanted a high school sweetheart. Maybe Azrail will be it," I say. "Together forever and ever."

"That is so delusional. I love it." I roll my eyes at Rosalie's words.

Nothing wrong with being delusional.

❀ ❀

"You're late, Aisha."

"Sorry, professor, I have a note," I say, handing it to him.

I smile at Azrail and make my way to my seat, only to trip on someone's bag and fall on my face. The class starts laughing, and I feel two hands helping me up.

"Are you okay?"

"Yeah, I'm fine. Just a little embarrassed," I mumble. "Thank you, Calvin."

"Aisha, go to the nurse's office so they can check on you."

"I'm fine, professor. Just a little fall. You can just email my parents about the incident," I tell him before walking to my seat, Azrail looking at me with worry.

I smile at him and hold his hand.

"I'm sorry I didn't come to help. I jus—"

"It would be too dangerous," I finished for him, giving him a warm smile. "I'm fine, Turtle."

I focus on the front of the classroom. Calvin was looking at me with a look I couldn't explain. When Abigail noticed, she scowled at him and made him turn around.

Weird.

"Today, since it's the first day back from Thanksgiving break and I don't want to work, you and your partners can talk about your projects or whatever. Remember, the first draft is due December 10th."

I turn to Azrail; he's still looking at me with concern in his eyes.

"Azrail, I'm fine, I promise."

"I know. It's just that..." He lowers his voice. "She tripped you."

Oh.

"It was probably an accident."

"Does she know?"

I nod.

Just because Abigail knows about my condition doesn't mean she would intentionally harm me.

Right?

"I don't like her."

"I don't either, but what can you do? Just focus on graduating."

He nods, but his cheeks were still red with anger. I squeeze them. He turns to me in shock.

"Sorry, couldn't resist." I laugh. Now his face is red with embarrassment.

"So, what do we have left to do?"

"We have to finish the last page of our report, and we're good to go."

"Okay, I can type it all out, and I'll send you the PowerPoint to look over."

"Perfect. After that, I can email it to the teacher, have him look it over before the due date."

"We work well together," I comment.

"It's because I'm awesome. What are you doing later today?"

"Practice and then homework."

"Let's go on a date. I already planned it," he says casually. My eyes widen in shock, I pull him into a kiss.

"I was not expecting this."

The date Azrail planned was by a river near the forest by the house we went to for our first date. There were fairy lights and everything for a picnic near the river. It's breathtaking.

"You don't like it?"

"I love it, Azrail. It's so beautiful," I gush, looking at the stars. We already had our picnic, so now we're just laying down and stargazing.

"Aisha, there's something I need to tell you."

"Yes, Turtle?"

"You've been honest with me all this time, and it'll be unfair for me to not tell you about my past. You deserve to know everything."

I nod, giving him his moment.

"This is something even my mother doesn't know about me," he starts, and I put my hand up, stopping him.

"Azrail, you're not obligated to tell me everything now—especially something your mother doesn't know," I say softly. "We've only known each other for a few months, and trust me when I say, I won't feel any type of way if you want to keep some secrets from me."

"But you told me about your past."

"Yes, I did. But I see the scars on your back and the emptiness in your eyes. I know your past is far more traumatic, and I want you to tell me when you want to—not because you feel like you need to."

He pulls me into a deep kiss.

"I really do appreciate you, Angel," he says, pulling away.

"I appreciate you more, Turtle," I say, pulling him back for another kiss.

Twenty-Two

AZRAIL

"Let's go in the water." Aisha says pulling away from me suddenly.

I nod.

She squeals and pulls off her clothes, and I follow suit. Usually I would tell her no because the water will be cold and even if she can't feel it, it's not good for her but we've been making out for the past fifteen minutes and her body alone is going to make faint.

The cold water quickly brings me back to life. I notice Aisha observes my reaction with a glint of curiosity behind her eyes. I smile and pull her close to me.

"How does it feel?" She asks.

"I don't know how to explain it, it's like having a nice dream and a bomb suddenly wakes you up." I try to explain, but it's hard to explain it to someone that has never felt it.

"Interesting, sometimes I wish I could feel things, but other times I'm glad, there are so many bad things in the world."

I nod.

I look down at her, the way the water drips off her skin and the moon makes her shine. She looks like a goddess, and I just can't bring myself to say anything.

"Why are you looking at me like that?" She finally says, looking down and smiling.

"Can't I look at you?"

She shakes her head and doesn't look at me.

I touch her chin and make her look at me. "You look beautiful Sunshine."

She smiles and gives me a peck on the lips before pulling back.

"Why don't you ask me?"

"Ask you what?" I ask, genuinely confused.

"About my Congenital insensitivity to pain? Why don't you ask me how it works when I hav-" She looks down without saying anything.

"When you what?" I ask, again, clueless on what she means.

"Sex? How does it feel? If I actually feel it? That's usually the first thing people ask?"

My eyes widen when she says that. I blink.

"Um well, I never thought of that Sunshine," I answered truthfully. "I've been focused on enjoying you as my girlfriend. I don't see you for sex, so the thought never came up."

"Oh."

"Don't get me wrong Sunshine, I am attracted to you, and I'm not going to lie and say you never turned me on," I say, pulling her closer to me. "If it wasn't for this cold ass water I would be dying right now, but I just worship you in a different manner that sex is a small thought in my mind."

She smiles and gives me another kiss.

"You really are out of this world." She says.

"Now that you brought it up though, I'm curious, how does it feel?"

"It's more mental than physical if that makes sense," She starts off. "My mind gets me off more than the actual action, I get horny and wet, but if my mind is not stimulated, then nothing."

"That's interesting," I say before picking her up and walking out the water. "It's getting cold."

"But I'm fine," She pouts, and I roll my eyes.

"Of course you are."

"I'm still sleeping over at your place tonight?"

"Yes ma'am." I say putting my hoodie on her.

Her parents aren't home often and she talks about how lonely she gets. I jokingly invited her to my place once, and it's been a recurring thing now. She sleeps on my bed and I sleep on a blow up mattress in the hallway.

"Let's go then, I miss your mom's cooking already."

"I'll make sure to tell your mom that,"

"They're best friends, I'm sure she knows."

We pack up everything and make our way to the car. Aisha falls asleep ten minutes in, and I'm left alone in my thoughts.

The way Aisha stopped me from telling her the truth about my past because she saw how it affected me amazes me. Deep down I really wasn't ready to tell her about my past, and I'm glad she noticed.

Aisha is truly one of the best things, besides my mother, that have ever happened to me. Her beauty, her kindness, her intelligence, and talent. She's my first girlfriend and yet, I feel like she will be my last.

There's no one like her, and for the first time in my life, I can't wait for the future.

※ ※

"We're home," I say quietly entering the kitchen with Aisha in my arms. She still hasn't woken up yet.

"I'm going to put her upstairs and then come down," I tell my mom and she nods.

"I left an extra bonnet on your dresser for her." She says smiling at us. I nod and walk upstairs with Aisha.

I lay her down and put on her bonnet, smiling as she makes herself comfortable on the bed, cuddling with my turtle.

I went back downstairs and greeted my mom. She was still in her scrubs and looked exhausted but still beautiful.

"Spit it out," She says, raising a brow at me.

"What?"

"Don't act clueless, the only time you act like this, looking at me with those puppy dog eyes is when you want to tell me something but you're too nervous to say it."

I laugh. "Mothers really do know everything, huh?"

Her eyes soften and she smiles sitting in front of me. "What is it?"

"I almost told Aisha my past today, including my name," I say softly.

She raised a brow at me, an indescribable emotion on her face. "Is that so? What happened?"

"When I was going to tell her, she cut me off and it wasn't time. She said I only felt obligated to because she told me about her past and that I'm not ready to tell her about mine yet."

"Smart girl, I like her." Mom says, smiling fondly.

"I do too."

"No, you love her."

"We just started dating mom, it's just appreciation at this moment." I say, trying to defend myself.

"Oh is that what kids are calling it these days?" She teases, raising a brow. "You both love each other, you were ready to tell her your name, and even I don't know that."

I stay silent.

Maybe she's right.

"It's getting late, go get yourself ready for bed, you got school in the morning." She says and I nod making my way out of the kitchen.

"Mom," I say, turning back to her.

"Yes love?"

"It's Asahi, my name is Asahi."

"Asahi, it's beautiful." She says softly, tearing up.

Twenty-Three

AISHA

I stare down at my boyfriend.

Boyfriend.

I love that word.

He's still sleeping, so I can examine his features without him shying away from me. The way his eyebrows are perfectly kept, his pale skin with a little bit of acne scar and his neck tattoos.

He looks heavenly.

His hair is starting to grow a bit more, meaning he's probably going to cut it soon since he hates when it gets too long.

"Why are you staring at me?" He asks, not even opening his eyes.

"How long have yo-?"

"Since the moment you got on this blow up mattress." He says pulling me fully on him and hugging me.

This man is truly something else.

"You're up before the alarm, why?"

"I don't know, just woke up." I shrug snuggling next to him. "You're mom already went to work and left us breakfast."

"That means I got thirty minutes left," He puts me next to him and uses the sheets to cover me before laying on my chest. "Let me enjoy it."

"Do you really enjoy sleeping that much?"

"I used to barely sleep until we started taking naps together," He answers, letting out a cute yawn.

I smile at that and let him fall asleep, playing with his hair.

As time goes by I start thinking about our futures. It's true that some people will stay with their high school sweetheart forever, but that's rare.

What if it comes to the point where Azrail only stays with him because I'm the only one he can touch?

What if we pick different colleges?

What if he gets tired of me?

What if I get tired of him?

"I can hear those gears turning, what are you thinking about?"

I look at Azrail, sleep still in his eyes but he was still looking at me intensely.

"I'm feeling a bit insecure."

"About?"

"Our relationship."

"Did I do something to make you insecure?" He asks, worry evident in his eyes.

I shake my head. "No, I was just overthinking about the future."

He wraps his arm around me and gives me a big hug. "Sunshine, let's live in the present. We both care about each other, and I don't see anything ending anytime soon."

"But,"

"No buts, I'm obsessed with you woman," he says, sending me his signature boyish smile.

"What about college?"

"What about it?

"What if we go to different colleges?"

"I'll follow you wherever you go, I never really had a dream school and I'm just going to go just to go," He says like it's the most obvious thing in the world. "Real estate doesn't really need a bachelor degree if you have the right connections."

"Bu-"

"No buts Sunshine, lets enjoy each other in the present."

"I appreciate you."

"I appreciate you more."

"Are you going to the winter formal?"

"I don't know, maybe."

Jamila, Calvin and I were in front of my locker socializing before first period. Even with the extra thirty minutes of fooling around, Azrail and I still made it to school early. Azrail went to class and Aisha decided to stay at her locker to talk to Jamila. Calvin joined a few minutes after.

"What, your boyfriend didn't ask you?" He says.

"Does your girlfriend know you're hanging around us?" I bite back and he shuts up.

The more time I spend with this dude, the more he makes me mad.

"Azrail seems like the shy one, you should ask him out instead." Jamila says, ignoring Calvin and I's bickering.

I know her and Calvin have been friends longer than us two, but I still don't understand how she manages to tolerate him. He's becoming more of a jackass every time I see him.

"I might, the thing is do I feel like going?"

"You should, I worked hard planning it."

"Fine, I'll go."

"And we can go dress shopping," She squeals, hugging me. "Are you coming, Calvin?"

"Abigail doesn't like social settings but I'll ask her just in case."

The bell rings, Calvin and I depart from Jamila and we make our way to class.

"Aisha, can we talk later today?" He asks me softly, I nod and make my way inside the classroom, sitting next to Azrail.

I started getting bored and spent fifteen minutes in class doodling while Azrail had his head down not paying attention. On the twenty minute mark, I tap his shoulder to get his attention.

I passed him the crumbled note in my hand.

You look hot, would you mind keeping me warm in winter formal?

He raises a brow at me and I smile, handing him a pen to answer. He rolled his eyes and answered the question, giving it to me.

Sure thing ダーリン *(darin)(darling)*

I look at the Japanese characters, no idea what they mean but I'll take it as a compliment.

The rest of the school day went by fast and slow. With the semester coming to an end, a lot of teachers are reviewing and letting us do independent study. Now I'm at Calvin's locker waiting for him to hurry up and tell me what he wants to say so I can leave.

I told Azrail to leave early and that I would stop by before practice. He was a bit reluctant to leave me with Calvin at first but he eventually left.

"Sorry I'm late," Calvin says, pulling me into a hug. "I walked Abigail to her car."

I roll my eyes and give him a pat on the back so he lets me go.

"What's up?" I ask him when we pull away. I noticed his eyes were fixed on my lips and I resisted the urge to roll my eyes.

"I just, miss you." He says quietly.

"Okay, is that all? I really have to go, I have practice."

"I'll walk you out."

I nod and start making my way to my car. I know he has more to say just not too much of a coward to say it so I decide to just wait for him to gain the courage he needs.

Once we reach the car Calvin takes my hand and slams me on the car door. My eyes widen, as he pushes himself on me and wraps his hand around my neck.

What the actual fuck?

He leans in to kiss me but I push my head to the side before he gets the chance. I'm frozen in fear by his action, I close my eyes and wait for him to finish.

"Abigail told me everything," He whispers in my ears. "You were so willing to open up your legs to a stranger and you dare reject me?"

He slams me on the car door one more time before he leaves. I stay there and collect my breath before entering my car and driving to practice.

Just act like it never happened and it'll be okay Aisha.

Just breathe Aisha.

Breathe.

"You're here early," Coach says when I walk in the practice room. She was the only one present and I sent her a smile.

"Just wanted to do some extra practice."

She nods and puts on some music. I started with my stretches, she was looking at me intensely but said nothing.

"Aisha?"

"Yes coach."

"Why ballet?"

She always asks me this when I'm not in a good mood.

"It's art, sophisticated, pretty, fun and challenging." I answer, finishing my stretches and starting my leaps.

"And?"

"It's magical, brings me to a fantasy world that allows me to forget."

"But?"

"I don't know." I lied.

"It's temporary and doesn't last forever." She reminds me, I roll my eyes.

I hum and keep going.

"Aisha remembers anything can be addicting, even dancing, it can become a drug that harms you in the end," She lectures. "Especially with your condition, your body won't even warn you when it's time to stop."

"I know."

"I'll let you practice today but if you don't solve whatever is happening with you soon, I will limit your practice because I will not have you kill yourself."

I nod before going back to my practice routine.

Just ignore and forget Aisha.

It'll be okay.

Twenty-Four

AZRAIL

I stare at my phone.

More specifically I stare at the message on my phone.

Once a whore always a whore.

It read with pictures of Ben on top of Aisha, leaning on her car. I block the contact and throw my phone on the wall. Cracking it.

I grab my cigarettes and lighter and walk outside. Aisha was supposed to come to my house before her practice but judging by the time, it's obvious she forgot.

I let the nicotine burn my lung as the pictures I saw burns in mind. In the picture they weren't kissing, so it could be out of context but my anger is not being reasonable.

Why didn't she call me?

I finish my first cigarette and take another one. If I was a normal person, I would be marching to Ben's house and fighting him, but I'm not normal.

Maybe I should go and fight him.

I look at my phone, no calls or messages from Aisha. She's halfway through practice, so I decided to go to her.

Throughout the whole walk, I managed to finish my pack of cigarettes and still felt the need for more. It's been long since I picked this nasty habit, the way it burned my lung was the only warmth I felt my whole life.

I arrived at Aisha's practice place faster than I thought I would. I decided to wait near her car instead of going inside and causing a scene.

An hour passed and I saw all of her classmates walk out except for her, it was getting dark and I was getting worried.

What is wrong with her?

Before I could make my way up I noticed a figure walking out, thirty minutes after her friends. Her coach seems to be telling her something, but her mind was somewhere else. I stay leaning on her car and wait for her to come to me.

It takes her a while to notice me, and when she does a fake smile sits on her face as she runs over to give me a hug.

"What are you doing here?"

"I missed you so much, I decided to come visit." I say, not mentioning the picture.

"I missed you turtle, I'm sorry I didn't come to visit, something came up."

"Is everything okay?" I ask, praying that she tells me the truth, but she doesn't. She pressed her car key to unlock it and I opened the door for her.

"Hurry up and get in so I can drop you home," She says, and I nod going to the passenger seat. The car ride was silent, Aisha just humming to a random song on the radio.

We arrived at my place and Aisha leaned back, closing her eyes before smiling at me. "Can I come in? I'm a little tired."

I nod, and we make our way into the house and in my room. I

gave Aisha a change of clothes to change into after her shower, I lay on the bed, not knowing how to act.

Should I just tell her I know? Why isn't she saying anything?

Half an hour later, she's back and crawls on the bed next to me laying on my chest. We stay silent, a tension between us and me not knowing whether to say something or not.

"Calvin tried to kiss me today," She says finally. "He offered to walk me to my car, saying he missed me and then forced himself on me."

I stay quiet and give her shoulder a supporting squeeze, feeling that she has more to stay.

"And when I didn't, he called me a whore and basically let me know that Abigail told him 'everything'."

I was now seeing red, murderous thoughts flooding my mind. I was pulled out of them when I heard a sob break from the girl next to me.

"I'm sorry," She cries. "I should've told you, I should've never met with him."

"Aisha, Sunshine look at me," I whisper, bringing her attention to me. "You did nothing wrong, absolutely nothing."

She nods, and gives me a weak smile. The mask she had on earlier, completely broken.

"Do you want to go report him together?" I ask softly, she shakes her head.

"What do you want? What can I do to support you Sunshine?"

"Hug me?" She asks softly, her voice weak. I nod and bring her closer to me.

"I'm going to kill that bastard and that bitch."

"I don't want that, let's leave them be. Please."

"Aisha, what he did was wrong. He deserves to be punished."

"I don't have the energy Turtle,"

I nod. Deciding to let it be, she's been through too much already.

"You know I'll always be here for you right?"

She nods and I give her a kiss on the forehead. We lay back down in each other's arms, sleep overcoming us.

∗ ∗ ∗

AISHA

I've been up for the past hour, watching Azrail sleep. My favorite activity. I never get tired watching him. His soft snores and the way his brows move as he sleeps.

He was adorable.

I originally wasn't going to tell him about Calvin to not stress him out, but a dam broke and I just felt that I needed to. His reaction to it was completely different from what I expected.

He was so understanding.

My thoughts got interrupted by his phone ringing, which also woke him up. He smiles at me and takes his phone out of his pocket, I couldn't help but notice the crack on the screen.

Where did that come from?

"Hello?" He answered in his sleepy voice. "I'm with Aisha, we were taking a nap."

He looks at me and mouths 'mom' before continuing his conversation, which mainly involves 'mhm's and 'okay's.

"What happened to your phone?" I ask and he shrugs.

"I'll tell you later," he says, giving me a kiss on the forehead. I nod and lay back down on his chest.

"Azrail,"

"Yes?"

"If you didn't have your condition, would you have noticed me?"

"You make it seem like it's an illness, it's a curse Sunshine not a condition."

I frown. "You didn't answer my question."

He chuckles at that.

"If I didn't have my 'condition' Sunshine, I would've asked you out the minute you walked into the school."

My eyes widened at his response.

"Really?"

"Yes, really."

"Simp," I tease and he laughs more. I look at him and smile, really enjoying the sight because something deep down tells me I will not be seeing it for a while. "I appreciate you."

"I appreciate you too Aisha," He says. "I don't know where I would be without you."

We stayed in silence for another twenty minutes, while I mustered up the courage to tell him what I really wanted to tell him.

"What's wrong?" He whispers, squeezing my shoulders.

I take a deep breath mentally preparing myself for his reaction.

"Don't freak out," I start off. "It won't be good for any of us if you do."

"Okay," He says, getting up and looking at me. Seriousness in his face.

"I need to go to the hospital, like right now before I die." I told him.

I see the gears running through his head but he says nothing. He got out of bed and got himself ready before picking me up and walking out the door with me, putting me in the car.

"Thank you for being calm about this." I praise him for not freaking out too much.

"We'll talk another time, trust me I'm not calm," He scowls at me. "Let's get you a check up first."

Twenty-Five

AISHA

"It's a good thing you came to the hospital, if you ignored this it would've become an issue." The doctor says, smiling at me.

I was dehydrated, a bit malnourished, and clinically exhausted. The stress of competitions and just focusing on my relationship with Azrail and that annoying Calvin, made me forget to take care of myself.

It wasn't until I was laying with Azrail and I started feeling tired that I knew that something was wrong. I've only felt that way three times in my life, and that was when I was close to dying.

"Did you call my parents?" I ask.

"The nurse has contacted your guardians the minute your boyfriend brought you to the clinic, they will be here later tonight."

"Thank you."

The doctor smiles at me and leaves. I look at a pissed off Azrail that's been standing in the corner of the hospital watching the whole process. He hasn't said a word since we stepped foot into the hospital.

"I'm sorry for worrying you, I really am," I apologize. "I didn't mean for it to get this far."

"Aisha," He said softly. "Baby, you can't ignore your health like this, this is very serious."

"I know, it's just, I wasn't thinking, I know."

"You can't be so careless Aisha, you can't just write everything off an 'I wasn't thinking' this is serious," He says, his voice getting louder and louder.

I start getting mad at him, I hate getting yelled at. "Don't you think i fucking know that Azrail, I've been told those words over and over again since I can remember." I yell back.

"WHY ARE YOU BEING SO CARELESS THEN?" He screams back at me. The tension in the room was thick, both of us fuming at each other.

"He does have a point," a voice interrupts us. I turn around, both of my parents staring at us.

"Not the time daddy," I comment, rolling my eyes, and Azrail says nothing except giving a bow ofrespect and leaving.

❧ ❧

It's been a week and the tension between Azrail and I is still there. He came to visit the first three days I was in the hospital, only for a few minutes to check how I was doing and nothing.

After I got discharged, he helped me and took me home but besides that nothing. None of us apologizing and it was getting irritating.

The winter formal was in a week and we are barely speaking to each other. I hate that I'm being stubborn but I hate that he's being stubborn too.

Why can't he just apologize?

"What's up with you guys?" Jamila asked, sitting next to me signalling to Azrail who went to get me food.

"He's mad at me for the hospitalization that happened last week," I answered with a small shrug. "And I'm mad at him for being mad at me."

"That's childish,"

"I know he is being childish,"

"No I mean you Aisha," Jamila deadpans. "You are being childish."

"What do you mean?"

"I mean Aisha, he is concerned about your health, it's not easy to be friends with someone like you."

"Ouch."

"You know what I mean Aisha, the constant fear of losing you just like that is painful," She explains. "We don't show it, but every time we get news that you are in the hospital our heart drops, and we prepare for bad news."

"Oh,"

"I know it's difficult and hard to forget sometimes, but Aisha, you are careless most of the time," She continues. "And for someone who is clearly in love with you like Azrail, of course he is going to get mad, because he cares."

"You got a point," I sigh in defeat. I look up to see Azrail walking over us with my food.

Even though he hasn't really talked to me, he has been taking care of me. Making sure I always eat lunch and drink water.

Now the guilt is eating me up.

"Why are you crying?" He asks in the same monotone voice he's been using since last week.

"I got to go," Jamila says walking away, leaving me and Azrail alone.

"I'm sorry," I pout a bit, tears still falling out of my eyes. "I should've understood your point of view more."

"And I'm sorry for yelling at you Sunshine," He says, wiping away my tears and giving me a kiss on the forehead. "I was just worried and concerned."

"I understand and you were right, I do need to be more careful, and understand how my illness also affects those around me."

"I care for you Sunshine and I really don't want to lose you," He says, giving me a tight hug.

❀ ❀ ❀

"Oh my gosh, you look so pretty." Jamila squeals and I smile.

"And so do you sweetheart," I smile at her, fixing my makeup. We both were getting ready for the winter formal, our dates picking us up in a few.

Jamila's date, a dude in her science class, is coming with her car and driving us to the dance. I originally wanted to bring my car, but he insisted. Azrail originally wanted me to meet him at his place, but my mom and Jamila wanted me to be home.

"Yall look so cute," My mom cooed when she saw us. "That blue looks amazing on your sweetheart."

"Thank you momma, where's daddy?"

"He had to go to the office."

"Of course,"

Before my mom could give me another excuse, the doorbell rang. I go and open it, taking my time instead of running towards the doorbell.

"Wow," My baby says, eyes wide.

"Wow yourself," I comment, drinking him in. He looked jaw droppingly gorgeous, I was in love.

He walks in and gives me a kiss on the cheek before giving my mom a bow.

"Good evening Azrail," My mom says, smiling at him.

"Good evening ma'am."

"I don't have to tell you the rules, it seems like you've been protecting this girl all on your own," She comments with a smirk. "She doesn't run down the stairs to answer doors anymore."

"Ma," I mumble embarrassingly. Azrail chuckles at the interaction.

"Let me take some pictures," Mom says, taking out her camera. I pull Azrail near the decorations to take a picture. "You guys are too cute."

Millions of pictures later, Jamila date came and took pictures with her before it was time to go to the dance.

We got to the dance a few minutes before the doors closed. Jamila and her date went to hang out with Calvin and I stayed with Azrail.

I didn't tell Jamila about the thing that happened with Calvin because I did not have the energy to go through the whole thing. Azrail was mad at first but understood where I was coming from and I was grateful for that.

Calvin and Abigail have been avoiding me and not giving me any trouble, and although I feel like it will not last, I'm enjoying the peace.

"Are you mad that we have to stay this far away from others?" He asks, snaking his arms around my waist. I smile, and give him a kiss on the cheek.

"All I need is you turtle, I love you."

He stops for a moment, looking at me intensely.

"I love you more Sunshine," He says, before pulling me into a deep kiss.

This man is going to be the death of me, and I'm loving every single minute of it.

Twenty-Six

AISHA

"E xcited about your performance tomorrow?" Azrail asks, feeding me one of his fries.

Since the break started, we spent almost every day with each other except when I have practice. We were both sad about me leaving to travel with my dad for a few weeks so we were making time for it.

My parents haven't been home for two weeks now and Jamila is in Florida living it up with her cousins. So it's just been me, and my man.

My man.

My man.

My man.

I love saying that.

"Aisha?"

"Hm?"

"You didn't answer my question Sunshine," He points out, making my cheeks burn up. "Are you excited about your performance tomorrow?"

I nod and smile at him. "Yes, and I'm so happy that you'll be coming."

"You've been zoning out a lot Sunshine, are you okay?" He asks concerningly.

"I'm fine, I'm just going to miss you so much," I complained for the fifth time this week.

"It's only for a few weeks, you were so excited about the trip with your dad."

"Not really." I admit.

"Really, I thought you would love the idea of hanging out with him," he asks, surprisingly.

He's right but the more I hang out with Azrail, the more I don't care for the old man.

I need therapy.

"Yeah but let's be honest, the more he keeps ignoring me, the more I want nothing to do with him."

"I'm sorry that you have to go through that Sunshine," He mutters, kissing me on the cheek.

"It's cool I plan on going to therapy to help, I'll be fine."

"Why don't you go to therapy now?"

"I don't want my parents to worry at the moment, plus I have a lot of things to do."

He pulls me into a deep kiss. I smile into it, letting out a breath of relief.

I didn't want to really tell Azrail that the reason why I haven't gone to therapy is because so far he's been the only therapist I need. When I'm with him, he fills me up with joy. I feel accepted, needed, and valued.

But that's a dependency and I don't want him to know that.

"I have a confession to make Sunshine,"

"What is it?" I ask sitting up, his face becoming red.

"I'm obsessed with you." He says bluntly, now it was my turn for my cheeks to get hot.

"Oh."

"It's becoming unhealthy Sunshine, I'm ready to kill for you, just say the word."

Not this again.

"I appreciate it Azrail, but you don't need to kill Calvin for me." I mentioned, knowing exactly what he was referring to.

"I won't have any regrets, believe me Sunshine," He mutters softly, his eyes holding no emotions.

Ever since that incident, something changed with Azrail. He has this murderous look in his eyes, all because he wants to protect me.

"Azrail, you're a human, you might not believe that, but you still have morals."

"Believe me Sunshine," he starts off, kissing my hand. "When it comes to protecting you and your safety, I have no morals."

Oh, wow.

🐢 🐢 🐢

"I love this time of year," Rosalie says smiling ear to ear. We were currently getting the final touch down on our hair, the show starts in a few hours.

I'm nervous and excited all at once. Azrail already came by and gave me a nice bouquet of flowers. I slept over at his place last night and had to rush to mine before he woke up.

After he brought me my bouquet of flowers, he left to get Jason and Saad since Jason's car had some issues. My mom and dad came with their own gifts, they're big gifts that everyone made a big deal about, but I liked Azrail's flowers more.

"Same, we look so pretty." I gush, looking at my outfits.

I look good.

"You guys look hot," a voice says interrupting us. I smile at that voice, while Rosalie blush.

"Thank you Jason,"

He smiles, giving me a single lilly and giving Rosalie a bouquet. These two are literally the cutest.

"Does this mean I'm forgiven?" He asks with a big smile on his face.

"Yeah right," I said, rolling my eyes. "You should've asked for my permission before proposing."

Azrail chuckles at our little back and forth. After Rosalie told me about Jason's proposal, I was happy at first and then got jokingly mad because Jason never asked me permission to marry my friend.

"Let me take you out to dinner to formally apologize." He teases, putting an arm around my shoulder.

"Hands off my girlfriend before I kill you."

We look at Azrail in shock. His face was ice cold, and tension was thick, he was not joking.

What is wrong with him?

Jason gives a short laugh and raises his hand in surrender, lighting up the mood. "She's all yours."

I smile and hug Azrail, while he says nothing. Azrail sometimes let his possessiveness out when we're alone. He has been protective and talked about hurting anyone who hurts me but never has he threatened to kill someone in public, and mean it.

"Relax turtle," I whisper in his ear, hoping that calms him down. "He meant no harm."

Azrail says nothing except kisses my forehead.

"Guests please make your way to your seat, the show is about to start." Coach says over the announcement, diffusing the tension.

"What was that?" Rosalie asks when the boy leaves.

I shrug. I wish I knew.

"Alright ladies, time to start."

We all start to rush to our positions, preparing for the performance of the year. Not only is it the end of the year performance, but it's also the time of year where dance agents come to start recruitment. Although I still plan to go to college, my dream to be a professional ballerina is still on the back burner.

A prima ballerina.

One can only dream.

The stage lights are on and the music starts, my heart starts to race. Excitement with a bit of nervousness and… fear.

What is he doing here?

Twenty-Seven

AZRAIL

"*They're pretty amazing aren't they?*" Jason says once the dance was over.

I barely heard him.

All I could do was nod, eyes locked on her. Aisha. My Sunshine.

There she was, center stage, moving like she was born to dance. Time didn't exist when she was up there. Everything else disappeared, the people, the noise, even the damn stage. It was just her. Glowing. Shining. Fighting something only I seemed to notice.

She looked... anxious. Her eyes weren't on the crowd. They were searching for someone. And when they landed on me, a wave of relief washed over her face, and over mine. I gave her a smile, subtle, thumbs up, the silent way of telling her: I'm here.

For the rest of the performance, her eyes kept finding me. She needed me to anchor her, and I couldn't lie, it made my heart ache and swell at the same time.

When the show ended, I clapped first. Loud. Proud. She blushed, and I loved that I could still do that to her.

While families ran to their dancers, I held back. I noticed Aisha slip out the back, away from the chaos. Quiet and unnoticed.

I followed.

The dressing room was quiet now. I found her near the mirrors, her back to me.

"Sunshine," I said softly, walking up and pulling her into me. "You were wonderful."

She didn't say anything, just melted into the hug like she needed it more than air.

I held her tighter. I knew something was wrong. I could feel it in my bones, the kind of wrong that makes your hands shake.

"What's wrong?" I asked, brushing her hair out of her face.

"Nothing," she mumbled, her voice barely above a whisper. "Just enjoying the silence with you."

Lie.

"Aisha," I warned gently. "I know when you're lying. Tell me what's wrong."

She opened her mouth — then a crowd stormed in.

"You did amazing sweetheart," her mom said, grabbing her in a tight hug. Her dad gave her a kiss on the cheek, stiff and silent as always.

"You really did. Both of you guys," Jason chimed in, his arms around Rosalie, smiling wide.

"I overheard coach talking to the recruiters, and your name came up," Rosalie added, winking.

Aisha squealed, jumping in excitement. Her mom hugged her again. Her dad? Just watched.

"I'll be waiting in the car. Dinner's in an hour," he said, then turned to leave.

"Can Azrail come?" Aisha asked him softly.

He didn't answer. Just gave me that look. The one dads saves for boys like me.

"Ignore him," her mom scolded, smacking her husband lightly. "We booked for everyone. Jason, Rosalie, their families. And you, of course."

"Thank you, ma'am," I said, nodding politely.

Then she turned to Aisha. "I'm guessing you'll be going with Azrail?"

Aisha nodded shyly. A small smile on her face.

Her mom winked and left. People started pouring backstage again, and I figured I'd give her some space. As I turned to leave, I locked eyes with Rosalie's cousin, Cindy, who threw me a flirtatious smile.

Gross.

The man beside her, the one glaring, didn't like me either. I could tell.

I ignored them, walking out.

AISHA

I was already shaking before I stepped on stage, but it wasn't the crowd or the recruiters.

It was him.

He was here. Antoine. My abuser. Sitting in the audience like he had no right to look at me, with Cindy. Both of them smirked like they owned me.

I wanted to vomit.

Why couldn't he just leave me alone?

My eyes darted through the crowd, searching desperately, until I found Azrail. His smile grounded me, pulled me back to earth.

There you are, I thought. He gave me a thumbs up and every-thing inside me calmed.

I finished the dance, my eyes glued to him when I could. I knew he noticed. He always does.

After it ended, I slipped out the back, away from the crowd, needing space to breathe. Azrail found me like he always does. He held me, told me I was wonderful. I didn't answer, not right away. I wanted to tell him everything, but I was scared. If I told him what Antoine did, he might actually kill him. And honestly? A part of me wanted him to.

"What's wrong?" he asked.

"Nothing," I lied. "Just enjoying the silence with you."

He saw right through me. Of course he did. But I didn't have to explain, because people barged in before I could.

My mom hugged me tight. My dad? Cold but present. Jason and Rosalie were proud. Rosalie even said she heard my name mentioned by the recruiters. I couldn't help but smile.

As things got noisy backstage, Azrail left.

Then she walked in.

Cindy.

She brought him.

I froze. Antoine's eyes were on me, searing through my skin. I couldn't breathe. Cindy smiled, that wicked smirk like she knew something I didn't.

"You did amazing, cousin," she said, ignoring me entirely.

I didn't wait. I ran.

Straight to Azrail.

"Can I get ready at your place instead?" I rushed out, not giving him time to ask.

He nodded, no questions. That's one of the things I love about him.

I knew he'd ask eventually, just not tonight.

Later, at dinner, I sat between Azrail and my dad, barely speaking. Mom, Jason, and Rosalie carried the conversation. I smiled when Rosalie teased me.

"I decided to get ready at Azrail's instead," I said casually.

Dad raised a brow at Azrail.

"Dad, relax. Nothing happened."

The table fell quiet again. I tried to eat, to pretend everything was fine, but then *they* walked in.

My father was on his feet in seconds. "What the fuck are you doing here?"

Mom looked equally furious.

"I brought my cousin Cindy... and her friend Antoine," Rosalie said, confused.

"I know who the fuck he is, and if he knows what's good for him, he better leave right the fucking now," my mother said sharply.

Jason leaned over to Azrail. "What's going on?"

I couldn't look at Azrail.

Cindy and Antoine walked off, Rosalie following after, trying to make sense of it. My parents sat down like nothing happened.

But it wasn't nothing.

Azrail looked at me, piecing things together. His jaw clenched, eyes darkening. I knew that look, we would talk later.

When Rosalie came back, she walked straight to me.

"I'm so sorry. If I had known, I'd have never allowed this. Aisha, I promise you'll never have to see them again."

Tears filled my eyes. "Thank you," I whispered.

"I knew we liked you for a reason," my mom added proudly.

Azrail didn't say anything, just squeezed my hand under the table. That was enough.

Rosalie leaned in again and whispered, "She told me everything. I don't believe her lies. I'm here whenever you're ready to talk."

Twenty-Eight

AZRAIL

I leaned against my car, arms crossed, waiting for her.

Aisha was still inside, talking to her parents. I wasn't in a rush, not tonight, but my mind was working overtime. I wasn't dumb. I saw the way Antoine looked at her. The way Cindy smirked. And more importantly, the way her parents reacted.

It didn't take a genius to put it all together.

Antoine wasn't just anyone. He was the one.

The one who hurt her.

And now I had a name. A face.

A target.

I looked up and caught her stealing glances at me as she talked to her mom and dad. She looked more relaxed than she did earlier, like something had been resolved. Her mom laughed and nudged her dad, clearly tipsy.

"Since you're going to be away for a while, you're allowed to spend the night with him tonight," her mom said.

Wait, what?

Her dad nodded, agreeing. "Yes. We saw how he acted

tonight. I believe that boy has the right intention. And if that turns out to be a lie… I'll deal with it."

Fair enough. I respected that.

Aisha hugged them goodbye and made her way toward me, smiling like she was trying to erase the tension. I opened the car door for her without saying a word and got in.

"I'll tell you everything," she said before I could even ask. "Just drive me home first so we can talk there."

I nodded and started the car. The silence between us wasn't uncomfortable. It was thick with anticipation, heavy with the truth she was ready to tell and the rage I was trying to keep locked away.

Her room was quiet when we arrived. Familiar. Safe. But the tension was louder than anything.

She sat on her bed and didn't look at me.

"First, I want to apologize," she said. "It was dumb of me not to say anything earlier."

"Tell me what?" I asked, even though I already knew. I needed her to say it.

"That my ex-abuser was here," she whispered. "That it was Antoine."

I felt it, that familiar surge of fury, but I kept it in check. Her guilt was louder than my rage.

"Sunshine," I said gently, sitting beside her. "Why didn't you tell me?"

She looked at me, eyes full of fear, but not of Antoine. Of something else. Something worse.

"I was scared," she said.

I pulled her into a hug, tightly. "I'm sorry that happened to you. But you never need to be scared again. I'm always going to protect you."

She froze in my arms. Then slowly pulled back.

"I wasn't scared of him, Azrail. Not entirely."

I blinked, confused. "Then who—?"

"Me," I whispered before she could answer. The words punched their way out of my mouth.

"You were scared of me."

I backed away from her, my heart breaking in real time.

"No," she said quickly, grabbing my arm. "Let me explain."

I stood frozen as she said the thing that haunted me the most.

"I'm not scared of you. I'm scared of what you'd do to him."

Her words knocked the air out of me.

"What do you mean?"

"You know what I mean, Azrail," she said, voice rising a bit. "After what happened with Calvin... you've been so protective. Reckless. You don't just want to defend me, you want to destroy anyone who threatens me."

"And that's a bad thing?" I asked, honestly confused. Didn't most people *want* that kind of loyalty?

"It's not bad," she said. "Not exactly. But you're not like everyone else, Azrail. You don't get to fight or punch or threaten people. One touch and they die. And you know that."

She was right. And I hated that she was right.

I didn't want to admit that part of me wanted Antoine to die. That it felt *right* — like I'd be restoring balance by ending him. But what would that cost?

"I'm scared of you getting caught," she said softly. "And taken away from me."

Before I could say anything, she kissed me, deep and soft and full of everything she couldn't put into words.

I smiled into the kiss. She wasn't afraid of my power. She was afraid of losing me.

When we pulled away, I said the only words that had been circling in my mind all night.

"I love you, Sunshine."

"I love you more, Turtle."

We kissed again, slowly falling back onto the bed, nervous but ready to take the next step, together.

🐢　🐢

AISHA

I didn't want to leave.

It was the morning of my flight with Dad, and I was wrapped around Azrail like I'd never see him again.

We'd spent the night together, not just physically, but emotionally. We finally had the conversation I'd been dreading, and for the first time in a long time, I felt *safe*. Like really safe. Like *home*.

"I'm going to miss you, Turtle," I whispered against his chest.

He stroked my hair gently. "Have fun with your dad, Sunshine. You'll be back in my arms before you know it."

He said it like it was a fact and somehow, I believed him.

"I love you," I murmured, pulling him into a long kiss.

The sound of someone clearing their throat ruined the moment.

Azrail's mom.

We jumped apart like kids caught doing something illegal. She smirked at us knowingly.

"Aisha, your mom called. If you don't leave now, you'll miss your flight."

"Yes, ma'am," I stammered, cheeks on fire. I gave Azrail one last hug and bolted out the door before she could say anything else.

As I disappeared down the stairs, I heard her behind him.

"Go wash up before you eat."

"Yes, Mom," he muttered, clearly still flustered.

"And Azrail," she added before he could leave, "please tell me you're using protection."

"Mommmmm!" he groaned, mortified.

I could still hear her laughing as I closed the front door behind me, smiling despite everything.

Twenty-Nine

AZRAIL

It's been 1 week, 1 day, and 19 hours since I last held Aisha.

Not that I was counting or anything.

…Okay, I was. Every second.

We tried our best to stay connected, but between the time zone difference and her dad running a tight schedule, it wasn't easy. Still, we made it work. Every morning I'd wake up to her pictures, her in new places, trying new food, laughing in sunlight that wasn't mine to bask in.

In return, I sent her long paragraphs and soft words for her to read at the end of her day. It wasn't enough. Nothing ever really is when you're in love and separated. But it was sweet, and it got me through.

I didn't expect to see her until the end of the week. So when the doorbell rang and interrupted my nap, I nearly ignored it. But if I missed one more important package for Mom though, I was dead. So I dragged myself to the door, groggy and annoyed, and then I opened it.

And got tackled.

"What the hel—" I choked out, and then I was kissed.

By the time my brain caught up, Aisha had already pulled back, cheeks puffed in frustration. "So you're not happy to see me?"

My mouth moved faster than my thoughts. "I am, Sunshine, you just surprised me."

She laughed, helping me up. "Sorry. I guess I don't know my own strength."

I pulled her close and kissed her the right way, deep, slow, breath-stealing. When we finally pulled apart, both of us grinning, the same words came out of our mouths at the same time.

"I missed you."

I didn't let go of her hand. "I thought you weren't coming back until the end of the week?"

"Dad had work, so we came back early. I didn't tell anyone… I wanted to surprise you first. And spend time with you before everyone starts dragging me to shop for prom dresses."

I raised a brow. "I feel honored."

"You should. You're getting VIP treatment, mister."

I smirked. "Thank you, ma'am. Let's go up to my room so you can tell me everything."

We laid on the floor, wrapped in a blanket. Aisha showed me pictures from her trip while I listened to her voice, the voice I'd missed more than I cared to admit. I didn't say much. I just watched her smile and soaked in every sound, every story.

AISHA

Being back in Azrail's room felt like exhaling after holding my breath for too long. I had missed this, missed *him.*

I showed him photos of Congo, the vibrant colors, the food, the markets, the people. And he watched me like I was the only thing that existed.

"Did I ever tell you why my dad takes me on these trips?" I asked.

Azrail shook his head.

"Besides the fun, he says that being African American... we don't always get to know our history like others. He wants me to learn about Black cultures — to see how extraordinary we are. How we thrive no matter where we are, no matter the situation."

Azrail smiled. "That's beautiful."

There was a pause, then I asked, "Can I ask something personal?"

He took a breath and nodded. "Yeah. Go ahead."

"Do you feel disconnected from your Japanese culture?"

He didn't flinch. He just nodded slowly. "Yes and no. My first adoptive parents whitewashed me. Didn't let me explore my culture at all. But when my mom adopted me... she made sure I learned. We took Japanese classes together. Cooked traditional food. Learned history."

He smiled softly. "I'm not fluent, but I'm better. I appreciate her for that."

I hesitated, then asked the question I knew might sting. "Have you ever been to Japan?"

"No. Not yet. I want to go... but I want to know more before I do."

I swallowed, carefully asking the next one. "Have you ever thought about finding your birth family?"

Azrail went quiet. Not in a defensive way — in a *resigned* way.

"My biological mom died during childbirth. My father passed before she knew she was pregnant. There were no other family members. I was put in an orphanage until I was six."

I reached for his hand. He didn't pull away.

"That's when a rich couple adopted me. At first, it was... fine. But as soon as the papers were final, they showed their true selves."

I stayed quiet. Let him speak.

"He abused me, the man. Emotionally and physically. The woman... just emotionally. I was 'the adopted help.' On my 11th birthday, he beat me so bad I blacked out. I prayed someone would come save me. The next morning, he came back — and this time, when he hit me, something happened."

I stared.

"He touched me. Then screamed. Died. Just like that."

It was like hearing a ghost story, except the ghost was real and sitting beside me.

"She kicked me out. I ran, ended up on the street. A few days later, Mom found me. Her husband had just been murdered by burglars. I... I killed them too."

I gasped quietly, covering my mouth.

"We didn't say anything. But from that day, we had an understanding. Her grief and mine... it clicked. She homeschooled me. Took me to therapy. Eventually, we moved here. I had enough credits to start high school."

I was crying by the end. Silent, real tears. I pulled him into the tightest hug I could give.

"You didn't deserve that," I whispered. "I'm so sorry."

He smiled into my shoulder. "Thank you, Sunshine."

"Your mom is amazing," I added. "Not everyone would do what she did. Not everyone would heal the way you have."

He nodded. "She's the first person who made me feel safe."

I kissed him softly on the cheek.

"I love you, Sunshine," he said quietly.

"I love you more, Turtle," I whispered back.

And in that moment, I knew, no matter what happened, no matter who tried to hurt me, I'd never be alone again.

Thirty

AISHA

There are two types of silence.

The first kind is calm, the rustling of leaves in the wind, distant chirps of birds, nature just... breathing.

The second kind? It's eerie. Still. Like the world is holding its breath before something explodes.

That morning, Azrail and I both woke up to silence, but not the same kind.

Mine was the peaceful one. His was not.

I woke up alone, like I usually do. No parents home, but I didn't mind. I made my way downstairs, the beads in my braids clinking with every step. On the phone with Azrail, of course. We didn't even talk. We just existed, side by side, through the line.

It was a new routine. But it was ours.

After breakfast, I told him goodbye and headed out for ballet. The car ride was quiet, not even music. My mind was too loud for that.

AZRAIL

I woke up before her, watching her sleep on my screen. We'd fallen asleep on FaceTime again. I always do that now, waking up first. I'd sit and just… listen to her breathe until she stirred.

I showered, dressed, and opened my sketchbook. Started working on a new portrait of her. I still hadn't gotten the eyes right.

Once she woke, we had breakfast "together," still quiet. Just being.

Then she left. I told her goodbye and grabbed my things.

I walked to school earlier than usual. The principal had emailed me about a meeting, but didn't say much else.

The streets were unusually quiet. That other kind of silence. The warning kind.

AISHA

Practice was quiet. Too quiet. Something felt off. Wrong.

I tried to push through, but I could feel it in my chest. When my coach dismissed me, I called Azrail. No answer.

That was it.

I went straight to school.

The second I walked in, the noise of a hundred conversations dropped. Eyes followed me. Whispers stopped.

Then I saw Jamila—pacing like crazy.

"Jamila, what's wrong?" I asked, already bracing for bad news.

She hesitated. "I know we don't talk about him, but... Calvin's dad. He was the victim of a hate crime. Last month."

My stomach dropped.

She kept going. "He's been in the hospital since. They think the guy was after Calvin, but... his dad was driving his car that night. They think it was a mistake."

She paused, too long. I knew where this was going.

"The cops came to question someone today. When he wouldn't give an alibi, they arrested him."

I closed my eyes.

"Aisha... it was Azrail."

I didn't cry. Didn't scream. I just turned and walked. Fast.

Jamila followed. She knew I was about to do something reckless—and I was.

As I made my way to Calvin's locker, the whispers rose again. Everyone watching. Everyone waiting.

Abigail was with him. Of course. They were too busy talking to notice me storming toward them.

"Calvin," I said loud and clear. "You know Azrail wouldn't do something like this."

He turned, surprised to see me.

"My dad's in the hospital, Aisha. I don't need your pity. Or defense of your weird-ass boyfriend."

Abigail smirked. "Why are you even here? Shouldn't you be off with your felon boyfriend?"

I inhaled. Controlled the urge to slap her into next week.

"I'm tired of your shit, Abigail. I'm not talking to you. I'm talking to Calvin."

She shut up. For once.

"Why would you think Azrail was the one who hurt your dad?" I asked Calvin.

"He jumped him," Calvin snapped. "Called him names. It's all on tape. You can't see his face, but from the build and clothes—

161

it's obviously him. And we both know your boyfriend's hated me for a long time."

"Oh, you want to go there?" I raised my voice so the whole hallway could hear. "Trust me, if Azrail wanted to kill you for *forcing yourself on me* a while back, you'd be dead."

Gasps. Silence. Staff started closing in.

"What's going on here?" a teacher shouted.

I didn't answer. I was already calling the one person I knew could help.

"Daddy. I'm going to the police station. I need help."

❦ ❦ ❦

AZRAIL

The cell was cold. And familiar. Not literally, but in that way where part of you always knew this day would come.

I'd always thought it would be something else. But hate crime? That wasn't just wrong….it was insulting.

I sat quietly, gloves on, face blank. No one had touched my skin—not even during the arrest. That was the only relief.

They'd questioned me earlier. Asked things I couldn't answer. Then they locked me in here.

I knew I had one phone call. But I didn't use it. Why bother? They didn't have anything.

"Follow me," an officer snapped, dragging me back to the interrogation room. Again.

He sat across from me, grinning like he knew something I didn't.

"You're a hard one to trace, Azrail. Everything about you starts at age eleven. But you slipped."

I stared back. Unimpressed.

"You got curious, didn't you? Went to an adoption agency to learn about your past. Had to use your current name. And guess what that brought up?"

He leaned in.

"Death follows you everywhere, Asahi."

I flinched.

Shit.

I kept my face still. "Can I use my one phone call?"

He smirked. He knew he'd hit a nerve. But I didn't care. I needed to call my mom.

Before he could say anything, another officer opened the door. "Sir, we have a problem—"

"Where the hell is my son!?"

That voice. Mom. And behind her, Aisha.

They didn't wait for permission. Just barged in, faces wild with rage and fear.

"Ma'am, your son is a suspect—"

"Shut the fuck up," Mom snapped.

"Leave it be, William," said the chief. Behind him, Aisha's dad had arrived with lawyers in tow.

The chief sighed. "Let the boy go."

I stood, raising my cuffed hands.

"You handcuffed my baby—"

"You handcuffed him!?"

Aisha and Mom shrieked in sync. The cops flinched. I laughed. Couldn't help it. These women were scarier than the damn charges.

The officer removed my cuffs. "Looks like you've got more support than I expected, kid. No wonder you didn't fold."

I rolled my eyes and immediately pulled Aisha into a hug.

"Thank you," I whispered, squeezing Mom's hand. "How did you know?"

"Aisha called me. Why didn't you?"

"I didn't want to worry you. And I didn't do it, Mom."

"I know, my sweet child."

"You can all go," Aisha's father said, his lawyers swarming. "We'll handle the rest."

I turned. My arm still wrapped around Aisha. She wasn't letting go anytime soon.

"Thank you, sir."

"No problem, son," he said, heading toward the chief's office.

But the officer I'd spoken to stepped closer.

"This won't be the last time I see you. And next time…"

He looked me dead in the eyes. "I'll be ready for you, Asahi."

Mom and Aisha froze at the name. I clenched my jaw.

I extended my hand. "See you around, sir."

He took it. Just barely. I was tempted to brush my skin on his but didn't… I think.

Aisha noticed. Her eyes flicked to me. But the guy didn't fall. So she said nothing.

"I love the hair, Sunshine," I whispered, adjusting my glove again. Then kissed her forehead.

Thirty-One

AISHA

"Baby, I can feel you burning holes in my head." Azrail says, putting his book down and looking at me.

"Sorry," I mutter softly, looking down at my own book. "Just got distracted I guess."

Azrail frowns and sits up, bringing me close to him and examining my face. He always knows when I'm hiding something.

"You know you can tell me anything right?"

I nod. I know I could tell him anything but I just didn't want to offend him. Ever since he got arrested a week ago, my mind is still not over that handshake he did with that officer.

When his mother and I asked about the officer, Azrail just shrugged, telling us how the officer did some research and found out his birth name and that we don't need to worry.

His mom did the opposite, she used her own lawyers and went to that adoption paper and now is now working on a way to seal Azrail's information and per Azrail's request, update the name on his birth certificate.

"I was just admiring your tattoos," I lied, trying to change the subject. "Do you mind coming up with a sketch for me?"

"Of course my love," He says getting up to get his sketchpad. We both know he doesn't believe my lies, but I'm very thankful that he decided to change the subject. "What were you thinking?"

"Um I'm not sure, can I look at your work first?" I smile at him as he hands me his sketchbook.

His sketchbooks were filled with beautiful drawings, some already transferred on his skin. I keep turning the pages, intrigued with the pictures until I land in one page.

"Oh wow,"

"You weren't supposed to see that until after I was done." Azrail mutters, getting a bit red.

"I love it," I awed, looking at the drawings. It was a portrait of me made with just a pencil but it looked like a black and white photograph. "What more do you have?"

I turn the page and gasps, it was sketches of me just doing random things, reading, facetime him, even a small sketch of me taking a nap. I kept flipping the page looking at all the drawings he got of me, and before I could flip anymore Azrail grabbed the book and stopped me.

"I think that's enough," He says, his face beet red in embarrassment making me laugh.

"Why I love them." I say truthfully, reaching for the sketchbook but he held it away.

"It's embarrassing."

"Are you saying loving me is embarrassing?" I fake pout, crossing my arms at him.

"N-no," He panics. I didn't think he could get any more red but I was wrong. "It's just too obsessive and I don't want to scare you away."

I smirk at his behavior and take the sketchbook flipping the pages. A small gasp escaped me. The page he didn't want me to see was filled with my name and his names, it seemed like he was trying to find the perfect font to combine them both.

"You're right this is obsessive," I admit looking up at him, he starts leaning away probably prepared for me to leave. "I love it."

I jumped on him, scaring him. He was on his back and I was straddling him, sketchbook in my hand.

"I think these are my favorite," I say pointing at some of the words. "Do you want to get my name tattooed on you? or was it just harmless sketching?"

"You really love it?" He asks, confused at my behavior. "You aren't creeped out."

"I mean, I can see why someone normal would be creeped out but turtle, I'm someone that's both touch and love starve, trust me, I love that you're obsessed with me." I tell him the truth.

Azrail laughs, shaking his head. "We both need help, I don't think this is healthy."

"According to who?" I say defensively, looking back at the sketches.

"Society?'

"Fuck society, you know what?" I say coming up with the perfect idea. "Let's tattoo our names on each other if we get married?"

"If? You mean when?" He says smirking up at me, making my cheeks warm up.

"I said if, so you could think you have a way out."

"I'm not going anywhere Sunshine, are you?"

"Not even in death," I mutter, giving him a big kiss.

"I want my name to be here," I say, pulling off his shirt and pointing to where I want my tattoo.

"I don't think I would be able to tattoo myself there," He chuckles.

"Um," He was right. It would be impossible for him to tattoo himself there. "Oh, why don't you teach me how to tattoo, and in the future we can just tattoo each other.

Azrail looks at me, his eyes clouding over with lust before he pulls me into another sloppy kiss and pulling away. "You just keep getting hotter and hotter, it's killing me."

* * *

"When are you coming back to school?"

Ever since the arrest, Azrail hasn't been to school. It's not shocking for him to miss so many days, but I miss hanging out with him. Jamila has been busy with catching up and college applications, since she procrastinates with everything and I had the terrible case of senioritis.

Calvin and Abigail still walked the school walls but with my outburst from last time, a lot of people avoided them and I was thankful for that.

"I'm not sure, mom says it's good to keep away so I don't get bombarded and harassed."

"Yeah, she got a point, who knows someone could try and fight you and it wouldn't be pretty," I say remembering Calvin threatening to fight Azrail if he ever saw him at school. If he touches Azrail, he would die on the spot.

"Yeah, so I'm trapped for everyone's safety, not even my own." Azrail chuckles coldly, my heart hurting at that.

"You got it all wrong turtle," I reassured him. "It's for your safety, because if anyone dies, your secret would be out and you will be in jail, and we both don't want that."

He nods and gives me a peck. "Come on, let's get dressed before my mom comes home and give me another talk."

I laughed and got ready with him. Once his mom walked in on us making out, innocently, and we got an hour lecture about safe sex. We weren't even sleeping with each other at that time, Azrail's reaction was hilarious.

Azrail's phone rang, interrupting the silence between us.

"Hello... um... oh... okay... keep me updated." He says before hanging up.

"What was that?"

"One of the lawyers, the officer that interviewed me died this morning so the process is being slowed down or something, he already contacted my mom to talk about next steps."

My blood ran cold at his confession. The way he said it so nonchalantly, he did not care for that officer died or really care about the case, it was concerning.

"Azrail," I said softly, preparing myself to ask him the question that's been on my mind for weeks.

"Yes Sunshine?" He asks, walking towards me, raising a concerned brow.

"D-did you um.."

"Did I what, love?" Concerned laced in his voice.

"Did you touch that officer?" I ask, cringing a bit when his face goes from concern to nothing.

Azrail steps away from me, shaking his head in disbelief. "He died of a heart attack, he had heart problems for a while now Aisha."

I flinch at his words, my eyes tearing up a bit. "I'm sorry, it's just that"

He steps back when I reach towards him. "Just what? Just that I'm capable of just murdering the man because he found out my identity? Is that what you think of me? A murderer?"

"No, n-no, Azrail, I-"

"I think it's time for you to go," He says, opening the door for me and stepping away from me, refusing to get close.

"I'm sorry," I whisper one last time before rushing out to my car, eyes burning with tears.

What was I thinking?

Thirty-Two

AISHA

It's been a week and I still haven't heard from Azrail. Instead of going to his place and checking on him, I decided to give him his space and wait for him to come to me first, and boy do I regret that decision.

Yesterday, a bouquet of red roses was sent to my house along with a happy valentines day card from Azrail. When I tried to call to thank him, there was no answer. He was still ignoring me.

My dad told me that the lawyers are working hard and Azrail will be off the hook soon, the police are already looking for other suspects. I don't know too much about the case because it's not my place, but since Azrail gave consent I get to know the basics.

"What's your mind?" My dad asks, bringing me out of my thoughts. I shake my head, I forgot he was there. Today was one of the days where he wasn't in a rush and could just stay home.

"Nothing daddy," I answered out loud when I saw the glare my mom gave me. "Thank you again for using your lawyers to help Azrail."

He gives a nod as a response before focusing his attention on my mom. I loved the way my parents loved each other, but hated it at the same time. When they're showing each other love, it's like everyone doesn't exist, including their own child.

Why did they even have me? I hope I never treat my kids like this.

"I gotta go, bye daddy, bye ma." I say getting up and cleaning my plate before going to school.

I debated on whether or not to go see Azrail. I miss our daily talks, his hugs, his presence. Before I knew it, I was pulling up in front of his driveway.

I ring the doorbell waiting for someone to open the door. I waited for what seemed like forever, in reality it was probably twenty seconds, for him to answer the door.

He looked breathtaking as always, today he seemed to actually be dressed up for school.

"Hi," I said softly.

"Hi," He whispers back, stepping to the side and inviting me in. My heart racing as I walk past him, tempted to go into his arms.

"I'm sorry." We both said at the same time once I walked into the house, both of us laughing at the interaction.

"I should've never accused you of something like that, I was just worried."

"I should've never kicked you out, that was rude of me, a part of me was just scared that you might've been right, what if I did touch him." He says, his eyes watering a bit. I pull him into a big hug.

"You're not a murderer, and I'm sorry for ever suggesting that you were."

He pulled back a bit from the hug, his eyes filled with sadness. "But Sunshine, I could be."

"But you're not."

"I could be Aisha, I get so mad at the thought of being away from you, that I want to get rid of all obstacles, what if one day I do kill someone."

"We'll cross that bridge if we get to it." I assure him, giving him a small peck on the lips before hugging him again.

"I missed you so much." He says, laying small kisses on my neck and squeezing the life out of me.

I smirk, looking up at him. "If you missed me so much, why didn't you contact me." I tease.

"I didn't think you would want to talk to me after the way I treated you, so I decided to give you your space and wait for you to reach me."

"I called you, nothing."

He smiles sheepishly at that, "Oh.. After our fight, I threw my phone and broke it."

"Another one, really turtle."

"But you got my flowers right?"

"Yes and I love them."

"I have more things planned for valentines day, I just wanted to do them when you weren't mad at me anymore."

"I was never mad, just worried."

"Let's go on a date after school and make up for yesterday," He suggested giving me a kiss before I could even answer.

I savor the kiss, missing his touch. Azrail always worries about chasing me away with his obsession with me, but little does he know I'm more obsessed with him than he was of me.

I never cared about him killing that cop, I was just scared at the thought of him being careless and getting caught. I don't want anyone to take him away from me.

He doesn't need to know that though, at least not yet.

"So you're going to school today?"

"Yes ma'am, mom said it's time to go before I stop caring about senior year."

"Tell your mom a big thank you for me, it's not the same

without you," I tell him. "Especially when we go to the college to work on that app we came up with, I see Rosalie from time to time so that's nice but working with those nerds alone is irritating."

"You don't appreciate being with your kind?"

"You know damn well you're a bigger nerd than me, now let's go." I say dragging him out of the house.

When we got to school, all eyes were on us. It's been like this for the past two weeks but now it's a bit more with Azrail by my side.

"Loverboy's back huh?" Jamila says leaning next to my locker, smirking at Azrail and I. "I take it y'all talking again."

I roll my eyes at her, of course she's gonna make it known to Azrail that I was crying to her about him. "Don't you have an assignment to complete."

"No," She says smirking. "I got three, get your facts straight."

I blink at her, no words coming to mind at her stupidity. Azrail laughs at our interaction, but it was cut short by an annoying voice.

"Oh so the racist finally comes out of hiding,"

I quickly step in front of Azrail, creating a barrier between Calvin and him, not wanting Calvin to keep his promise and try to fight Azrail.

"What do you want, Calvin?"

"Oh so now you remember my name, your girlfriend can't fucking protect you Azrail, my dad is on his death bed because of you."

"It wasn't him, Calvin, let it go." I yell back, annoyed at his behavior.

"Why are you fucking defending him, he got no alibi."

"Aisha don't." Azrail warns but I pay him no mind.

"Yes the fuck he does, he was with me that night," I yell out tired of Calvin's behavior.

Calvin looks at me in shock, and Azrail glares at me for telling the truth. Since the day he got arrested, I found out the day Calvin's father got attacked was the night I was with Azrail but he didn't say anything because he didn't want me to be a part of this mess and did not want out pictures used for the case.

"What's your proof?"

I pull out my phone, looking for one of the pictures I took that night, that includes the timestamp and date. It was a picture of me laying on Azrail, both of us shirtless, nothing exposed but anyone with a brain cell can understand what happened before that picture.

I shove my phone towards Calvin so he can see properly but before he could, Azrail snatched the phone out of my hand.

"Stop trying to be a fucking hero *Jake*, the police is taking care of everything, if I'm guilty let the law work," Azrail spits out glaring out him.

Calvin looks at me, "Be careful Aisha, death follows this one everywhere he goes."

I felt Azrail tense at Calvin's words. "Why don't you go spend time with your dying father, it's only a matter of days until you start visiting the cemetery instead of a hospital."

I gasped at Azrail word, it was filled with so much venom. The students surrounding us started muttering, throwing hateful words towards Azrail.

"You'll regret this." Calvin seeth walking away.

"That was mean," I scowled at Azrail.

"It was but he made me mad," He says, shrugging like it was nothing. I shook my head and opened my locker, knowing it was useless to talk about it.

The school day went by slowly, it was now the third period, one more period before lunch. I was walking in the empty hallway, walking to class after a bathroom break when someone popped up in front of me.

That someone being my turtle. "Hi love,"

"Why are you out of class, miss?" He questions giving me a peck on the lips.

"I should be asking you the same question," I retaliate.

"Fair enough, wanna ditch?'

"Can't," I pout, he does the same. "I got a calculus test today."

He rolls his eyes, "I can't wait for our date today."

"Me too, I love you,"

"I love you m-"

BANG !

I jump at the sound, my body shaking with fear. I looked at Azrail, tears in my eyes while he seemed on high alert.

BANG ! BANG !

Faint screaming could be heard and the sound started to come closer. I was frozen in fear, both of us were.

CODE RED ! CODE RED !

The alarm system in school went off, snapping Azrail out of his frozen state. Azrail grabbed my hand and started running towards the nearest shelter.

BANG ! BANG !

The sound seemed to be getting closer, by now Azrail had picked me up, my face buried in his chest while he ran to find shelter. I physically could not react, still frozen in fear. I've seen stuff like this happen in the news, but having it happen in real life, nothing could have ever prepared me for that.

Azrail managed to find a small room and push me in before closing the door behind him. It was a janitor's closet, and it was dark, perfect for a hide away. I couldn't see Azrail but I felt him, he was holding on to me, his breath a bit shallow laced with fear like mine.

BANG ! BANG !

I bury my head on his chest.

"It'll be okay Sunshine," He whispers in my ears, groaning a bit but I paid no attention to mind just accepting his comfort.

An hour passed before I heard police sirens, Azrail was quiet, his arm still wrapped around me in a comforting manner. Thirty minutes passed before someone tried to open the closet door, when they weren't successful they started walking off.

It wasn't until I heard Jack and his fathers voice walking away that I opened the door. The hallway was surrounded by cops and scared students.

"Jack" I yell at their retreating figures. His father both turn around and look at me, like they have seen a ghost.

"Princess are you okay? Where are you shot?" Jack rushes up to me, examining me.

"What are you talking about? I didn't get shot." I say.

He looks at me, confused by my behavior. He and his father start to approach me slowly. "Aisha, are you okay?" His father asks.

"Were you by yourself during this whole ordeal?"

"I'm fine, Azrail protected me." I say raising my hand to point at the closer but stops when I notice the crimson red substance in my hand.

Oh no, did I get shot?

Jack opens the closet door wider. Azrail was still in his sitting position, blood pouring out of him, his eyes closed.

I froze staring at my boyfriend, he was paler than usual. He did everything to protect me, and I was so scared I didn't even realize he got hurt.

"Aisha? AISHA???????????? AISHAAA?????????" I hear Jack call out for me while his father radioed someone.

"Don't touch his skin, he's germaphobic." I whisper to Jack before everything faded to black.

Thirty-Three

ASAHI

Today is a calm day. I haven't spoken to Aisha yet because my phone is still broken and mom says I have to get a new one myself. I'll eventually get around to it, I just haven't had the time.

I stare at the drawing of Aisha, my Sunshine. My beautiful Sunshine. The portrait was coming out exactly like her, the misplaced curls, the round face and yet sharp features. I frown, something didn't feel right.

Something wasn't right.

"Asahi, breakfast !!"

I put down my sketchbook and make my way downstairs. "Morning mom," I say, giving her a small kiss on the forehead before sitting down to eat.

"When is Aisha coming?" She makes small talk.

"In a few hours, I finally managed to finish the painting of her, can't wait to show her."

Stop being in denial.

"That's nice dear," She says, giving me a small smile. I nod and continue to eat, trying to my mom who was just staring at me, unmovingly.

Wake up.

"Everything okay mom?" I ask.

"Of course my love," She said, giving me a small smile but still not eating. "You've just grown so much."

"Mom, I know I'm leaving for college soon but that doesn't mean I will be leaving forever."

Her eyes tear up, like always. "My only wish was to see you grow up, find love, and live your life, I'm so proud of you Asahi."

My side starts to hurt again, making me crouch over in pain. Mom does nothing but just stand there looking at me.

"Mom, help." I cry out, reaching out for her.

"I thought I had more time, I guess not." She says solemnly before kissing my forehead.

I woke up inside a void, memories of what happened at school flooding back to me.

Aisha? Where is she?

"This girl really is the only thing you think of." The voice says.

"Is she okay?"

"She's fine, you managed to protect her," She coos, touching my cheeks, I flinch still not used to her cold hands. "But Azrail, we need to have a serious conversation."

"What? Do you have another gift to give me?"

"Azrail, your love has been making you careless,"

"What do you mean? I always stay covered and try not to touch anyone."

"You got hurt Azrail, you were always careful, if I didn't intervene every single officer and first responders would have died trying to save your life."

"Isn't that what you want anyways? You're the one that cursed me in the first place, you should've just left me for dead."

"I didn't curse you child, I saved you," She says softly. The scenery around us changing.

"What do you mean to save me?" I ask, looking around at the new environment. It looked familiar but I couldn't pinpoint where it was exactly.

"Where is that goddamn brat?"

That voice, it can't be.

We were in a different room in the house. I watch as the monster walks towards a little boy cowering in the corner, me. I flinch as the monster raises his hand to hit the boy.

"You were destined to die that day," The voice says, freezing the vision. "I saved you."

"I beg the moon and the stars to give me the power to protect you,"

"Why? Why do you care?"

"Have you not realized this by now sweet child," The voice says bringing herself into the light. She was a short and thin Japanese woman, her skin was so pale that it looked transparent. "I'm your mother."

I back away from the woman, not knowing what to say. I keep examining her, trying to find the features of her that look like me. The thick black hair and nose was similar, but that didn't mean anything.

"That's impossible, my mother is dead."

"Come on now Asahi, you kill everything you touch, you are speaking fluent japanese right now, and talking to your dead mother is what's impossible to you."

I stay quiet, she has a point, all of these are illogical and yet are happening.

"Are you an angel then? Or a deity? How does this work?"

"Those are answers that would take a millenia to answer and understand, it all depends on your beliefs, every culture would give me a different name." She explains. "Just think of me as your guardian angel, an energy that is here to protect you, to make you happy."

I sit down, holding my head as I feel a migraine forming.

"I know this is too much for you to handle Asahi and I'm sorry for ever putting you in such a situation," She says crouching in front of me, her hand coming to my face to wipe my tears.

Instead of flinching away, I let her this time.

"What do I do now?" I ask, my voice low, barely a whisper.

"Come with me to the light my son, everything will be alright." I take her hand and follow her into the light, a light so bright that there was no darkness.

Everything will be alright.

※　　※

AISHA

It's been a month since the shooting at school.

A month since Azrail saved me.

A month since Azrail first fell into a coma.

Within that month, he coded two times in the operating table.

Became septic after his first surgery. Coded once again. And is now on life support.

The school shooter was someone who graduated last year, not a lot of people knew him nor the reason why he did what he did.

He was a "normal kid", apparently, he wasn't an outcast or extremely popular. There's still an ongoing investigation, the police want to be certain he wasn't working with anyone else.

"Aisha, sweet child, go home." Azrail's mom says, putting her hand on my back in a soothing manner. I say nothing, closing my eyes and listening to his faint heartbeat.

My routine consisted of going to school, sometimes practice, and laying next to Azrail waiting for him to wake up. His mother will come to his room every time she's on break or before she starts her shift.

She sighs, giving Azrail a small kiss on the forehead, her eyes tearing up. "I've always dreamed about giving him affection, but never did I imagine a situation like this."

That day when Jack found me and Azrail and I fainted at the sight of him, paramedics helped him and he went straight to surgery. When I woke up and when his mom found out what happened, we were shocked at the lack of casualties surrounding Azrail.

As of now we're both assuming it's because he's unconscious, his mom took advantage of giving her son attention but after a while, we just wanted him to wake up. No matter what the results after that are.

"You have one hour before closing, make sure you leave without a fight this time."

"Thank you ma'am."

She nods, giving me a kiss on the forehead and walking out to start her mi

The hour passed like a second before it was time to go. I left without a fight this time, not wanting to cause trouble for anyone today. Like the past few months, the drive home was a blur.

My mom had food on the table for me, dad tried small talk so I could open up but I stayed quiet. I eat to make them happy, do my homework, and fall into a deep slumber waiting for my love to wake up.

Thirty-Four

AISHA

"Aisha, come down!" my mother called from downstairs.

Her voice was shaky. I could hear it in the way she said my name. My chest tightened, the way it always does when I can feel something bad coming, but I pushed it down and kept getting ready. I was planning to go see Azrail, and nothing else really mattered.

Still, I made my way down, dragging my feet. As soon as I hit the bottom step and turned into the living room, I saw both my parents standing there. Faces tense. Eyes darting. Like they were afraid of me.

"What's wrong?" I asked, already irritated. I didn't have the energy for family drama, not today.

"Honey," my mom said softly. "There's something we need to tell you before you leave."

Something in the air shifted. I felt it wrap around my shoulders like ice.

"Is everything okay?" I asked, even though I already knew it wasn't. I was suddenly wide awake. Alert.

What happened to Azrail?

"It's about Antoine," my mom said gently, reaching out to guide me to the couch.

Antoine?

I hadn't thought about him in weeks. Months, maybe. Not with everything else going on. Especially not after... well, after Azrail.

"What about him?" I asked, wary.

"He's been arrested," she said. Her voice broke, her eyes glassy. "He was abusing Rosalie's cousin. A neighbor called the police, and they caught him... in the middle of it."

I froze.

My first reaction? Relief. A dark, guilty kind of relief. The kind that made my stomach twist even though my brain screamed *finally*. I just nodded. Didn't say anything.

"That's good," I muttered, standing up. "I'm going to see Azrail now."

I didn't get far.

"There's more," my father said, blocking my way. "The family... they're asking if you'll testify in court."

I didn't even think about it. "I'm good."

"Aisha!" My mom's voice cracked with disbelief.

"I don't want to drag my shit back into the light," I said sharply, grabbing my bag. "The past is in the past. They have evidence. Let that be enough. I want out of it."

"We need to talk about this, young lady," my dad said firmly, stopping me again.

I closed my eyes. Counted to three. All I wanted was to see Azrail, sit next to him, hold his hand in that too-quiet hospital room.

"There's nothing to talk about," I said through clenched teeth. "I just want to go."

Then he snapped.

"Goddamn it, Aisha! Can you stop thinking about that boy for one damn second? Focus on what matters! He's not going anywhere, but you—*you*—you have a chance to finally bring justice to your abuser."

The air was sucked out of the room.

Even my mom flinched.

I slowly turned to face him, something inside me boiling over.

"That boy?" I said, voice shaking but not from fear. "That boy is the love of my life. That boy has been there for me more than you ever have. That boy has shown me real love—real care. Not the kind of love you throw at me with money and trips you cancel for 'emergency meetings.'"

"Aisha, watch your language," my mom whispered.

But I wasn't done. Not even close.

"You want to talk about justice? Let's talk about how you two only ever loved *each other*. I was always the extra. The afterthought. You would've saved one another in a fire before even *thinking* about me."

I could feel tears burning behind my eyes, but I didn't let them fall.

"I spent my entire life watching your love story from the outside, begging for scraps. And if you had been better parents—if you had seen me, really *seen* me—I might not be as fucked up as I am right now."

The silence was suffocating.

I looked at them one last time.

"Now, if you'll excuse me," I said, stepping past them. "I'm going to see the person who's lying in a hospital bed—because he took bullets for me. Something neither of you would've ever done."

And with that, I walked out.

❦ ❦

"You've been awfully silent." Azrail's mom says coming into the room.

"Just thinking." I answer, mind still flooding with conversation I had with my parents earlier.

"What about?"

"A conversation I had with my parents earlier." My outburst surprised all of us. I didn't think I would have said all of those things to them, it all just came out.

"Your mom did tell me you were upset," She says sitting next to me, and giving me a comfortable pat on the back. "I'm sure you guys will patch it up soon."

"Any news on him?" I ask her, changing the subject.

"Doctors are suggesting pulling the plug."

My heart sank at her words. With all the times he had coded, and medical complications a part of me knew this would be brought up, but hearing it out loud...

"I could pay, I have access to my trust fund now that I'm 18, please don't pull the plug." I beg, feeling my throat closing up, tears falling out of my eyes.

"Aisha, breathe for me,"

I follow her instructions as she talks me out of the panic attack I was about to have.

"I'm not pulling the plug on my baby," She reassures me. "I just wanted you to be aware of how serious this is, he might not wake up."

I shake my head, sobbing into her arms. "He will, he will."

We stay silent, quietly crying into each other's arms. The thought of living without Azrail starts to become more and more a reality, the hope slowly fading. Once his mom left, I took out the stuff I bought for today.

The pictures of use I had printed the other day, just countless selfies I forced him to take with me. Some off guard ones, and some "off guard" ones that I made Rosalie and Jamila take for me. Next was our college acceptances, his mom didn't have the heart to open his and I was waiting for all of my letters to come.

"I got my final letter today," I spoke out loud to him. "I figured it was time to open them, since decision day is next month."

"You know, I never realized you applied to all the schools I did, you stalker."

I opened the letters one by one, not surprised that we got accepted to all of the schools we applied to. Azrail got full rides to majority, and I got scholarships that covered basically half of my tuition.

"I know you said you would follow me wherever I go, but it would be very nice if you can just wake up and make the decision yourself."

"I miss you turtle, the world seems bleak without you. I miss your warm hugs, your soothing voice, I miss everything. Please wake up."

By the time I did something I haven't done in a while. I got on my knees and begged the universe, pleading for Azrail's life.

"Please wake up."

I don't know how long I stayed in that position but eventually I fell asleep. The sound of the machine beeping and someone shaking me.

"What's going on?" I asked Azrail's mom, standing up suddenly when I saw the three doctors in the room.

"Miss, I need you to step out for a moment while we deal with this." One of the doctors says touching my shoulder and ushering me out.

"You're not pulling the plug are you?" I asked, trying to see what was going on but the doctors were surrounding Azrail and I couldn't see anything.

"Miss, please stand outside." The doctor says again, clearly in a rush to go to his colleague's side.

"It's okay Aisha, they're not pulling the plug." Azrail's mom says, grabbing my hand and walking to the waiting area with me.

"What's going on?" I ask her again, anxiously looking at the closed door to Azrail's room.

"I'm not sure, there was some activity in the machine," She says, squeezing my hand.

I suck in a deep breath. Last time there was activity, he was going into cardiac arrest and almost died. That's when they finally put him on life support.

Half an hour later a doctor walks out, looking at us with an empty expression on his face. My eyes break with tears, while Azrail's mom asks questions about her son.

The doctor's answer had her sinking on her knees while a sob broke from me as I made my way to the room.

Thirty-Five

AISHA

The Patient has woken up.

Those were the doctors' words.

When those words left his mouth, I rushed to the room while Azrail's mom cried and thanked the doctors.

He was lying there, still connected to some machines but it looked like he was able to breathe on his own and that's what mattered.

He did not see me come into the room, he was still laying back while the doctors checked on him. I noticed that the doctors were able to touch him without any issues, which raised concern.

Universe, please don't let this be a false alarm.

I walk up to him, the doctors give me a nod of permission to get closer.

"Turtle," My voice cracks as I touch his hand. It was warm, comforting. More tears fell out of my eyes as I felt him weakly squeezing my hand.

"Sunshine," he whispers, his voice cracked and dry, a side effect of not drinking water for two months.

"Shh," I whispered back when I saw he was struggling to speak. "Don't overdo it."

The nurse that came into the room handed me water with a straw and I gave it to him as he slowly drank.

"My baby," His mom sobbed out, finally walking into the room and sitting on his side opposite of me.

"Mom," he whispers, his voice a bit clearer.

"Can we hug him, doctor?" I ask, feeling like holding his hand wasn't enough.

At his nod of approval, I give Azrail a big, but cautious hug. My body is finally relaxing after months of stress.

"I love you so much," I whisper.

"From the looks of it, your son seems to have made a great recovery, it's a miracle." I heard the doctor explain as I was hugging Azrail.

"We will keep him here for tests and to watch over him," another doctor added. "If everything goes well, he will be dismissed by the end of the week, the earliest."

"Thank you, doctor."

"We'll leave you be."

The doctors left the room as I pulled away from the hug.

"Mom you can touch me now, give me a hug," Azrail says, reaching out to his mom who was still sobbing. I step back and watch the reunion between the two.

Mrs. Morris, hugged her son with all her might, praying over his head. I watch the scene as they make up for years of affection. A tear left Azrail's eyes as his mom hugged him.

"How?" She asks him, pulling away and fixing his hair.

"This is going to sound crazy," He says, giving her a shy smile. "My birth mom taught me how to control my powers, now I can choose who I harm."

"Baby, I've raised you for years, trust me, what you just said sounded completely normal to me." She says with a small laugh.

"Don't ever do anything this stupid again," I yelled and softly hit his arm after he pulled away from his mom.

"How long have I been out?" Azrail asks with a small chuckle.

"Two months," I answered.

"I'm sorry for worrying everyone, but Sunshine, if I had the choice I would do it a million times over if it meant saving your life."

"I don't care Azrail, you were on life support, the doctors wanted to pull the plug." I sob.

"Good thing I have you two to protect me," He jokes, making me roll my eyes.

"I'll go talk to the doctors and nurse about your care as you stay in the hospital," Mrs. Morris says, giving me a squeeze on the shoulder and a kiss on her son's forehead. "You two catch up."

We watch her leave. I turn back to Azrail, tears falling out of my eyes again.

"Please don't cry my Sunshine," He coos, wiping my tears. "I'm okay, everything is okay."

"I really thought I lost you Azrail, I don't know what I would've done if I did," I admit.

"You would've moved on, live your life and be the amazing woman that I know you are." He says in a firm voice, holding my face.

"I don't think I could've," I admit. "I felt empty without you Azrail, I wanted to join you."

"Let's not think about that now," He says, pulling me on his chest. "I'm alive, you're alive, we're alive. Let's just enjoy this moment as if nothing happened."

"But something did happen Turtle,"

"I know love, and we have a lifetime to talk about. Let's just enjoy each other's coming now."

"Why are you so cheerful?"

"Aisha," he says, letting out a sigh. "For the first time in my life, I was able to touch and feel my mother's embrace, and I have the love of my life by my side. Why shouldn't I be cheerful?"

I stayed quiet, scared to say what I wanted to say out loud.

I've read books and watched movies about patients being cheerful and fine, moments before death. What if that's how he is feeling right now?

The universe let that be a myth. Please let him be okay.

❦ ❦ ❦

"You're quiet." Mrs. Morris says sitting down next to me.

They took Azrail out for testing a few minutes ago, and we're in his room waiting for him to come back.

"Hm, I guess I am," I mumble, my mind racing with thoughts.

"I know what you're thinking," She says again. "You're wondering if he is experiencing *Terminal Lucidity*."

"If there's a term for it, that means it's a real thing," I mutter, shrinking more into my seat.

"It's extremely rare, and I understand your fear."

"I don't want to lose him."

"When my husband died, a part of me died with him, being Azrail's mother gave me something to live for," She starts. "I don't want to lose him either, but I'm not going to sulk around while he's awake."

"You want me to act like I'm not scared?"

"I want you to live in the moment with him Aisha, I want you to enjoy every single moment you have with him, without worrying if he's going to die or not."

"How?"

"Be delusional, Azrail literally could end lives with just a touch, he miraculously woke up from a coma," She praised. "Nothing about that boy is normal, he defies all odds of nature, it's time to be delusional and believes he isn't going to die. Believe that he spent those two months training with his birth mother who died 18 years ago, and can now control those magical gifts."

"He really is a special case." I let out a soft laugh, feeling better after her speech.

"And his love for you, the love you have for each other is out of this world, he will be fine. You guys are going to live life together, get your dream jobs, get married, and give me grandkids."

I laugh at that, another deeper laugh joins us.

"Don't you think you're asking for grandkids a bit too soon Mom?" Azrail says as his nurse wheels him into the room.

"Just talking about the future." She shrugs, helping him on the bed.

"How are the results?" I asked the nurse.

"Passed with flying colors Sunshine," Azrail answered with a cheesy smile. "I can be discharged in two days, and be back to school by next week if I want."

I looked over at the nurse who nodded in agreement.

I smiled, hugging him tight. "Perfect, that means you won't miss decision day."

"I'll go wherever you go, love, it doesn't matter to me."

I rolled my eyes at his response, not surprised by it at all.

"What else have I missed?"

"The person who attacked Calvin's father has been identified and is in jail, trial is next month. As for your case, we can proceed and sue the people that arrested you or not. Your choice." His mom said.

"Leave it be, I don't feel like going through that process."

She nods and walks out, leaving me and Azrail alone in the hospital room.

"Jamila and Saad have something going," I say, trying to make the conversation more lightheaded.

"Wow, and their parents are okay with that?" Azrail says referring to the age gap.

I shake my head. "Jamila plans on telling them after graduation, they've just been talking about nothing serious."

He nods, "What about you Sunshine?"

"Besides spending time with you, I worked with Rosalie on our class project, even though we were excused, I found joy in developing an app, we got a B- on that."

"Really? So I'm guessing you want to be a computer science major?"

"Yeah, that means I really do need to get better at math." I fake sob, making him laugh.

"Aisha."

"Yes,"

"I know there's something you're not telling me."

I let out a sigh, "You know me so well."

"What's happened, love?"

"My abuser got arrested, I'm being asked to testify, and got into an argument with my parents about that." I let out one big breath.

"Wow," Azrail blinked. "That's a lot to unpack, do you want to talk about it now or later?"

"Can I not talk about it at all?"

He shakes his head.

"I was stressed out and wanted to come see you and my parents bombarded me with the information, and I just went off on them. I told them how I truly felt."

"What about Antoine? Do you want to testify?"

"No, I don't want to reopen that chapter in my life. Does that make me a bad person?"

"No Sunshine, you don't owe anyone, if you don't want to testify you don't have to."

I pull him into a kiss.

I feel his hand wrap around my waist, pulling me closer. The kiss deepens with desperation from us both. We finally pull away from our breath when the door opens.

Our moms were standing in the doorway, my mom with a bouquet of roses. I pull away from Azrail, not acknowledging her.

"Your mom told me you were awake and I came as soon as I could."

"Thank you, ma'am,"

There was an air of awkwardness in the room, my mom and I avoided eye contact with each other. Azrail and his mom are trying not to point out the obvious.

"Aisha, can we talk?" Mom asks, out of respect for Azrail and his mom I decided to not cause a scene and follow her out

"I'm sorry for how we treated you," Mom said the moment we were in a hallway alone. "I didn't realize how much it affected you."

"Where's dad?"

"He's at work."

"Of course," I scoff. "You know Mom, I used to think he was a cheater one time. I thought he used to neglect both of us but then I realized how he was only held up in the office whenever it concerned something with me. And how he was always too busy to receive guests at work but when it came to you, he had a separate room in his office just for you."

"Aisha,"

"Don't," I stopped her. "It's obvious how much he loves you and detaches himself from me. And you're no better for trying to justify his actions."

"Aisha, he does love you," She sighs. "Look, you have every

right to feel the way you do. Your dad is extremely emotionally closed off, he detaches himself from anyone he thinks he might lose in the future."

"That's not fair for me."

"He had a hard past, lost a lot that he cared for and he just detaches himself. He cried with joy when I was pregnant with you, excited to hold his baby girl in his arms. He painted and decorated your nursery himself. Your birth was traumatic for both of us, at one point he had to make the choice between you and I. When he thought he lost me, he tried to hurt himself, blaming himself for the decision he made."

"Oh."

"When the doctor told us about your illness, and how you have a low lifespan, he detached himself even more. I'm not justifying his behavior, but rather, explaining it. I wish he was better but therapy and pills can only do so much. Please forgive him."

"I'm sorry that he had to go through that Mom," I responded." But my feelings are also valid, and I have every right to feel the way I feel about you both right now. He learned to love you, he could've learned to love me though, but he didn't, because he was a coward."

"Aisha."

"And I understand he's the love of your life. I tried to see your position, tried to imagine the situation with me and Azrail, and I know for a fact I would not stand for that type of behavior. I would have made sure that my child got the proper love they deserve. No matter how much I love their father."

"Let's go to therapy."

"Family therapy didn't work last time, it's not going to work this time. But I'm willing to work this out and find a nice middle ground. No amount of therapy and money will make up for how I was treated."

"I understand. I'll be staying with your father tonight, so make sure you go home and get some rest on your bed."

I nod and walk away to Azrail's room. Settling next to him and zoning out as he and his mother give me space, continuing their conversation as if nothing happened.

Thirty-Six

AZRAIL

Today was my discharge day.

Finally,

I couldn't wait to get the hell out of this hospital. Every beep, every nurse walking in with another chart, another question, it all made my skin itch. I missed my bed, my sketchbook, and Aisha. God, I missed her.

She couldn't come pick me up, though. AP exams were around the corner, and she had to be in class. I understood, but it still stung a little. Thankfully, Jason and Rosalie offered to pick me up. Mom was working another long shift, and I wasn't cleared to drive yet.

Jason was already waiting outside when the nurse wheeled me down. He'd been solid—like, real solid—the past two months. Showed up when Aisha couldn't. Hell, he even yelled at me for not calling him the second I woke up. I deserved that one.

"Surviving death really has changed you, huh?" Jason said the second I hopped in his passenger seat.

I smirked. "What do you mean?"

He laughed, like I was the biggest idiot on the planet. "First the hug."

"Hey, I almost died. I was happy to see my friend."

"Now you're admitting we're friends out loud?" he teased, one brow raised. I rolled my eyes and looked out the window.

"Lastly, you asked me to tattoo you."

"Well, there are some places I can't reach myself, and I just want my tattoos to look right."

"Hm, sure," he said with an eye roll.

I gave his shoulder a squeeze, catching him off guard again. "Look man, I almost died. I saw my birth mom in a coma. I *know* I'm acting differently. I see the way Aisha and my mom have been watching me. But I'm good, I swear. I'm just… appreciating life."

Jason looked at me sideways like he wasn't quite convinced, but he didn't press.

"I see," he finally said. "But you were gone for two months. This change, it's jarring for everyone."

I nodded. That made sense. For me, it felt like sleep. A weird dream with my mother's voice in it and a strange sense of clarity when I woke up. But for everyone else, it was grief. Waiting. Hoping.

"Does your newfound appreciation for life mean you'll work at my shop now?" Jason asked, hopeful.

"Why not?" I shrugged. "I need to start making some money anyways."

Jason gave me a look. "You got some big plans you want to share?"

I smiled—coy, knowing. "Maybe. You'll find out soon enough."

He chuckled. "I love this new you. Yeah, it's a little weird, but you're more open. Now the friendship doesn't feel one-sided."

"It was never one-sided."

Jason looked at me like he didn't believe me, but he didn't argue.

🐢 🐢 🐢

AISHA

The bell rang and I didn't wait a second. I grabbed my bag and shot out of that classroom like my life depended on it.

"*Aisha, wait for me!*" Jamila's voice called out behind me.

I slowed just a little, still half-speed walking to my locker. I couldn't hide it—I was excited. Azrail was finally home. And all I wanted to do was see his face and hold him close.

"What's up?" I asked as she caught up to me.

"Can I get a ride home? My car's still in the shop."

"What happened to Saad? He usually picks you up."

"We broke up."

I stopped mid-step. "Oh. I'm sorry." I pulled her into a quick hug, surprised when she leaned in and didn't let go immediately. When she stepped back, her eyes were glossy.

"It's alright. I'll be fine."

"Why'd it end?" I asked gently.

She hesitated. "People kept talking about our age difference... and it got to him. He ended it."

I didn't say anything at first. I *did* think the age thing was weird, but it was never my place to say it out loud. Her parents liked him. If they'd met later, it wouldn't even be an issue.

"That must be hard," I said, trying to offer comfort. "Do you want to spend the day together?"

Her brows shot up. "You sure you don't want to spend time with Azrail?"

"You're my friend, Jamila. I care about you too."

She gave me a soft smile, the kind that said she needed that more than she realized.

"Let's stop by Azrail's first," I added, unlocking my car. "Then we can have a girls' day. I've got a whole breakup kit ready."

She sniffled. "Thank you."

"Don't mention it."

The ride to Azrail's place was quiet, but comfortable. As we pulled up, I spotted him outside with Jason. They were leaning against the porch railing, smoking and talking, looking like they hadn't a single worry in the world.

I stepped out and crossed my arms. "I take it your mom's not home yet?"

Azrail turned to me with that sheepish smile that made me forgive him for just about everything. "She won't be back till the morning," he said. "We got the whole house to ourselves."

He was teasing, but I wasn't here for that. "Actually," I began, glancing back at Jamila. "I was just stopping by for a second. Jamila's heartbroken and I'm spending the day with her. Is that okay?"

His face fell for half a second, just enough for me to notice before he pulled it together. He walked up to me and pressed a kiss to my forehead.

"Spend some time with your friend. Tomorrow, you're mine."

I giggled, a little warmth bubbling in my chest. "Deal."

I gave Jason a quick smile and turned to jog back to the car.

"No running," Azrail called behind me.

"Dude, you are *so* whipped," I heard Jason laugh.

I didn't care. Azrail was home, he was safe, and he was still mine.

Tomorrow, he'll have all of me.

Thirty-Seven

WEDNESDAY

AISHA

"Everyone is staring," I whisper to Azrail.

"They always stare," He answers unbothered by the news. He was leaning on my locker waiting for me to get my stuff out before we walked to class.

"Yeah, but this time it's different."

"How so?" He asks, opening his eyes slightly to look at me.

"I don't know, they seem like your biggest fans."

He rolls his eyes and pulls me close to him. "Are you jealous, Sunshine?"

I hit him softly. "No, I'm just not used to it."

"They're just curious because of the events that happened last time I was here, it'll all blow over by next week."

I nod. He's right, if someone else were in a coma after the school shooting, I too would be staring at them when they come back.

"Did you make your decision?" He changes the subject. I sigh and shake my head.

Decision day was in three days and I still wasn't sure what school I wanted to go to. "I want to do ballet, want to try and become a prima ballerina but I also have a joy for app development, so computer science is in mind."

"Why not do both?"

"Is that possible?"

"Sunshine, you are smart and capable of doing everything and anything, I don't see why you don't think you can do both."

"But that's a lot of time and money and stress and,"

He pecks me on the lips to stop my ranting. "College is stressful, that's true, but it never hurts to try, you are lucky enough to have a family that can afford your dreams."

I nod. "But what if I forget myself, what if the stress is too much and I neglect my health."

"I won't let that happen," he reassures. "And you don't have to do both right away, maybe start with one and slowly ease your way to the next?"

I gave a quick peck on the lips, the bell interrupting us before it went any further.

"Time for class,"

"We can always skip," He smirks and I shake my head.

"I think you've had enough of a break from school."

He nods agreeing with me and we both make our way to class, hand in hand. The morning classes went by faster than expected. Teachers leave us alone to study or work on projects for the end of the year, they were done teaching for the semester.

"You got less work than I expected," I commented looking at Azrail's workload.

We were currently in the library during lunch hour. I was studying for my AP calculus exam doing the study guides the teacher provided while Azrail worked on his missing work.

"Instead of making me do every minor work, the teachers prepared packets of the important stuff to work on. Next week I have exams to see if I understand the courseload."

"What about your AP exams?"

"I don't think I'll be taking them."

"Why not?"

"I don't really need them for my major, and I don't mind retaking some core classes. Less stress for me."

"Fair enough," I sigh, going back to my workbook. After a while, I feel Azrail hands on my shoulder.

He starts giving me a massage like he always does when I'm stressed. It doesn't make a difference physically, but the action and thought behind it calm me down.

"I love you."

"I love you too Sunshine, so much."

❦   ❦

SATURDAY

Today is decision day and I still haven't picked a college.

Azrail was next to me, providing me with emotional support as I scroll through social media reading our classmates' decision-day posts.

Jamila was going to Columbia University in New York, majoring in biochemistry. Calvin was going to Howard majoring in engineering and Abigail is going to some school, I didn't care to finish reading her post.

"Are you really going to wait for me to pick before you pick your school?"

Azrail nods. "I'll follow you wherever you go, Sunshine."

"And if I pick a ballet school are you going to learn ballet for me?" I tease, smirking at him.

"I'll go to one of the schools that's near that school. I applied to a lot of schools Sunshine."

"You're so obsessed with me."

"I am."

"I think I'm ready to make my decision," I say with a big sigh, clicking on one of the tabs to make my final decision.

After doing so, I let out a breath I didn't know I was holding. Azrail holds me close to him and gives me a kiss on the forehead.

"I'm so proud of you," Azrail praised before going to his computer and picking his choice.

We both close our computers and face each other, a series of emotions running through our eyes.

"So you're really going to follow wherever I go," I state.

"Forever and always."

"We're growing up, graduation is in two weeks."

"The world isn't ready for us."

"They aren't Sunshine, they aren't," He echoes, giving me a kiss on the lips. "Now go get ready for the barbecue."

Jason and Rosalie were hosting a small barbecue, to announce their engagement and Azrail's well-being. They invited us and our family to join the celebration, but we were already running late because of my decision day breakdown.

After getting ready I went back down to Azrail who was waiting for me patiently. I gave him a once over, my man looked fine. His hair was freshly cut, and he was wearing all black.

"Damn," I muttered looking up at him and licking my lips. "I got a fine boyfriend."

I watch as the tip of his ears turn red, a small smile coating his pink lips. His eyes were filled with love, and lust as he pulled me into a hug, his hand drawing circles on my back.

"I got a fine girlfriend."

"Maybe we should go upstairs, we're already late, a few more minutes won't hurt."

"Rosalie will kill us."

"She'll understand," I say, grabbing his hoodie and pulling him upstairs to my room.

"No running," He says, picking me up and throwing me on his shoulders, his long legs getting us to my room in a few seconds.

As he drops me on my bed softly a squeal leaves my lips, which was cut short by his lips dominating mine.

Thirty-Eight

AISHA

MONDAY

F inals season.

    Students of all grades dread it, some more than others.

I was one of the students stressing out, while Azrail was completely fine.

Not only is my boyfriend a genius, but he somehow doesn't know the definition of test anxiety. And unlike him, my normal exams and my AP exams are in the same week.

Lucky bitch.

"You're going to be fine Sunshine, you know the material." He says trying to calm me down, I roll my eyes and push him slightly trying to focus on the study guide.

"Easy for you to say," I grumble while he and Jamila laugh.

"Why are you so worried anyways Aisha, it's not like you're taking the calc exam today."

I froze at her words, panic coming over me while her eyes widened when she realized what she said.

"Shit, I'm sorry." She spews out trying to apologize, I close my book and get up.

"I'm going to class," I mutter, making my way to where my AP lit exam was being held, hoping I can get a few minutes of silence before the test starts.

After a tiring 2 and a half hours, I walked out of the classroom drained and less anxious. I don't feel confident with my performance but it was done and out of my control now.

I smiled at Azrail who was leaning outside of the classroom with a bag of food and my favorite drink order.

"Sorry for my attitude earlier," I apologized, taking the drink from him and giving him a kiss on the cheek. "I was just stressed out."

"No need to apologize Sunshine, I understand." He says giving me a soft peck on the forehead.

"You're the best," I mutter enjoying his embrace, all the stress flowing out of me. "Why are you here anyways? There's no exams for you today."

"I'm here for emotional support and this," He says, pulling back and opening the box he held in his hand.

It was a donut themed proposal, cute and simple.

"Aww," I cooed, giving him another kiss on the cheek. "It was already an unspoken agreement but I love it nonetheless."

"The rest of your gifts did not get here yet," He says, biting one of the donuts.

"There's more?"

"Of course there's more, you deserve the world Sunshine."

"Cheesy much."

"Only for you."

WEDNESDAY

Today was the last finals for Azrail and I.

I was done with AP testing yesterday, and like I predicted AP calculus almost killed me.

Today was a fun day, for me anyway. Azrail and I were going to present our app to our computer science class, and then afterwards I had a short performance for my theater class.

Unfortunately for Azrail, his AP chemistry and Biology teacher are making him take an exam since he opted out of his AP tests.

Some teachers are too much.

"Aisha, Azrail, are you guys ready to present?" Our professor calls out, we nod and make our way up front.

"For our app, we decided to make something fun and educational for people who have trouble studying like me." I said jokingly, earning a few chuckles.

"We decided to take inspiration from olden applications such as Duolingo, Coolmathgames, from pass generations to come up with 'Learningo'." Azrail says, raising a brow at me with the names.

I never said I was good with coming up with app names.

I rolled my eyes at Abigail who scoffed at the name, "The name is a working progress, the brain of the project wasn't available when I was coming up with the name." I say shutting her up with a glare.

The presentation went smoothly afterwards. Azrail explained the logistics of the game since he was 100% present for the first part of the project and I talked about the process of making the app in college.

"Any questions?" I ask at the end.

"Do you have proof of the app working?" The professor asked, pointing out the fact that we didn't provide proof on the PowerPoint.

"Yes, my calculus grades from before and after I started using the app is the proof we used," I admit sheepishly. "I was just too embarrassed to show the whole class so I included it in our final report."

Azrail gives him the report and we watch as he flips and briefly reads over the report. He nods approvingly, a small smile appearing on his face.

"Why the turtle as a logo?" Someone in the class calls out.

"I just love turtles," I shrug and smile at Azrail.

"Good job, please stay after class." Our professor says dismissing us to our seats.

I wonder what he wants to talk about.

"You did amazing Sunshine," Azrail whispers to me and gives me a small squeeze on my hand.

Once the bell rang the students left and it was just Azrail and I with the teacher.

"I must say, I am very proud of you two for coming up with such an application." He compliments.

"Thank you sir, but it was all Aisha."

"Don't listen to him," I comment feeling a bit embarrassed. "Azrail helped a lot with the ideas, I mainly did the coding and design with help of the college students."

"You guys are an amazing pair, are any of you interested in making this a career?"

"Aisha is," Azrail says softly, pushing me toward the professor.

"Is that so? What about dancing?" He asks, genuinely confused.

I don't blame him, I was always late in class because I put ballet as a priority.

"I'm doing both," I admit. "Going to the School of American Ballet while also doing online classes in NYC, as a computer science major."

"Wow," he comments in awe. "That's a lot but I have faith you can do it, your parents must be proud."

I stay quiet. I haven't told my parents about my choices yet. Not because I don't want to, but because I haven't seen them in a while.

"I'm also very proud of her, my girl is going to do big things." Azrail says, putting his arm around my shoulders comfortingly.

I blush at that comment.

"Here is mine and my brother's card, whenever you're ready to start an internship and learn more about app development, please contact him and tell him I sent you. You show great potential and I can't wait to see how far you go Aisha."

I feel my eyes water as I take the card.

"Thank you professor."

Thirty-Nine

AISHA

FRIDAY

Today is prom day.

If someone told me a year ago that I would be going to prom with the love of my life, I would laugh in their face.

I would go on a rant about me not having time to entertain high school boys, and not having the energy to buy overpriced tickets in order to attend a pointless school dance with people I don't like, wearing an overpriced dress that I will probably only wear once.

But here I am, in front of the mirror, wearing a dusty blue sweetheart mermaid dress, with a nice slit to show off my legs. Hair in a low ponytail and silver heels.

The dress was simple, not over the top, and something I know I will wear again.

I look gorgeous.

My thoughts were cut short when I heard a sniffle. My mom

and dad were standing in front of my door, Mom was crying, it looked like my dad had some type of emotion on his face.

"Aw mom, why the tears?" I ask walking up and give her a hug.

"You look, beautiful sweety, I'm so happy you decided to enjoy your senior year, with all of the shit that happened."

I wipe away her tears and look up at my dad who hasn't said anything. He clears his throat, giving me a jewelry box. I gave a small smile and opened it, it was a pair of earrings.

"Thank you, Daddy," I give him a quick peck on the cheek before backing away.

"Your father has something to say to you, I'll go downstairs and entertain the guests."

I didn't have a big prom sendoff but since my house was the biggest, the group decided to come here for pictures. I was the last one to get ready so no one has seen me yet.

I sit on my bed silently examining the gift my dad gave me, I feel the bed dip and my dad clears his throat again.

"I'm sorry I haven't been the best father." He spoke after a few minutes of awkward silence. "And I'm sorry for what I said about your boyfriend."

"It's alright."

"I don't have a proper explanation to justify it, and you have every right to be mad at me," He continues. "I do love and care for you Aisha, you're my only child, my only daughter."

"I know you care."

"You don't have to lie, I know that I don't show it in the proper way, and I know when it comes to the people in my life, I make it painfully obvious that your mom is first." He admits.

I stay silent.

"And that does make me a bad father, no matter how many gifts and trips I give you, I know that doesn't make up for it. I was an absent father and you don't deserve that. I won't go into much detail, since I know your mom already talked to you about our past."

"Yeah, she did."

"But Aisha, I do love you, I do want what's best for you and I do want to protect you. It's hard for me to feel emotions and when I do they're strong, the thought of losing you will simply break me. No matter how obvious it seems on the outside, your mom is not the first person in my life. You both are, you are my blood, my joy, and the thought of losing you affects me every waking moment."

I don't say anything. Waiting for him to finish.

"I will try to be better in the future, I won't let the thought of losing you cripple me from loving you, since it's obvious that I already started losing you with my actions anyways. I have started more intensive therapy, and stronger pills, and will work less so I can be more available for you. Your mom and I have talked, we will be more present in your life, promise."

I give him a big hug, not knowing what to say.

"I love you, Daddy,"

"I love you more my sweet child." He responds, giving me a tight hug.

We pull away from the hug and I put on my earrings, ready to go downstairs. My hand is on my dad's arm as we make our way out of my room.

I smiled at Azrail who was looking at me intensely once we reached the top of the stairs.

"That boy," My dad mutters. "Love you a lot, borderline obsessed with you, I see it in his eyes."

"Huh?"

"He has a craziness in his eyes when he looks at you, the same one I have for your mother, probably even worse," My dad says in a warning voice. "Those fires in his eyes show me he will kill for you, no matter the consequences and although I am happy that you found someone to protect you, be careful."

I say nothing to my dad's warning, instead, I put on a big smile and walk towards Azrail giving him a hug.

A low whistle comes from Jason.

"You look gorgeous Aisha," he compliments, giving me a smile.

"Thank you,"

"OMGGGGGGGGGGGGGGGGGGGGGGGGGGGGG"

I cringe at my best friend's squeals and face Jamila who was wearing a beautiful green prom dress. It incorporated her culture and had nice intricate details of gold.

"YOU LOOK SO GORGEOUS" We both squeal at each other, making everyone in the room laugh as we run towards each other hugging and complimenting each other.

"Picture time," Rosalie says, getting in between us and taking pictures with her camera.

We made our way to the living room, taking pictures and chatting. Azrail's mom and I were obsessing over how we looked, and embarrassing us by planning our wedding. I ignored the way my dad was looking over Azrail and me, his words in the back of my mind.

"You look, gorgeous Sunshine," Azrail whispers in my ear while we are taking pictures. I look up at him, fixing the tie on his suit.

"You look handsome, turtle."

Forty

AZRAIL

SUNDAY

"Are you almost done? I'm running late."

"Maybe if you sat still it would go by faster," Jason yells back at me.

"I'm just not used to someone else tattooing me," I say in an apologetic tone.

Today Jason had free time to start making the tattoos I had planned. Unfortunately, he can't do it in one sitting so we are starting off slow. He was filling in the places I couldn't tattoo on my chest, with flowers and leaving a nice spot for future portraits.

I plan on surprising Aisha with the tattoos I'm getting. I know I promised to teach her how to tattoo me but she's been busy and I got a bit impatient.

Plus the tattoos I'm getting all correlate to her, I got ballet shoes, her favorite flowers, and even a small turtle. My next

216

session with Jason will be the portraits I drew of her, I just don't know where I will get them yet.

I really am obsessed with my girl.

"You really are obsessed," Jason comments, looking through my sketchbook trying to recall what I asked him to do. I'm thankful he can freehand and not fuck my shit up.

"Damn right," I answer back, closing my eyes and letting the sound of the machine soothe me. That didn't last long before Jason was handing me my ringing phone.

"Hello,"

"Hi, turtle are you busy?" A smile coats my lips as I hear my Sunshine voice.

"Just at the tattoo shop is everything okay?"

Jason rolls his eyes at the change in my voice, I ignore him and focus on Aisha.

"Yeah everything good, just wanted to hear your voice,"

"I miss you too Sunshine, how was practice?"

"It was fine, coach talked about my weight but I just ignored her, it didn't impact my performance at all, you're still coming to the award show tonight right?"

"Wouldn't miss it for the world."

"And afterward we're still on for our date?"

"Everything is booked and ready, I just need to pick up your gift and all is set."

"Would I have time to go home and change for our date?"

"Yes, I made sure to prepare for that."

"You are perfection," she praises. I feel like my cheeks heat up at her compliment.

"I gotta go, Jamila, Rosalie, and I are going to do some last-minute grad shopping. See you in a few hours."

"Goodbye, Sunshine."

"Whipped as hell," Jason says laughing and I roll my eyes at him.

❀   ❀

AISHA

I look in the mirror doing some final stretches as we prepare ourselves for the award ceremony.

The end-of-the-year ceremony was something small, no big performance, just a nice goodbye to the students who are moving up from the company. Only 4 out of 30 of us are deciding to go to a dance school, and not stay back.

I was the youngest in the group who decided to go, people like Rosalie usually keep going to this company while they're in college for something else before moving up. That way they can still learn but in a manner that accommodates their school schedule.

Because I was the youngest, all eyes were going to be on me. And for the first time, I was not nervous. Because I know Azrail is going to be in the crowd, along with my parents.

I look over the flowers on the dresser. My dad came extra early and dropped off some flowers for me before going to the audience. They weren't my favorite, but at least he's trying.

"I got a surprise for you," Rosalie whispers in my ears.

"You're pregnant?" I ask jokingly.

She says nothing. I look back at her eyes wide.

"YOU AREE"

"Shhh," She says and nods excitedly. "I just found out last night."

"Does Jason know?"

"No not yet, I plan on making it a nice surprise."

"I'm so happy for you," I cooed, hugging her tightly while she laughed. "I'm going to be an aunty."

"Wait, what about ballet?" I ask pulling back.

"It was more of a hobby, I don't want to become a prima like you so it's fine, but do keep it a secret, I want to make sure everything is okay with the doctors before making it a big deal."

I nod, "Understood, can I tell Azrail? He's good at keeping secrets."

She laughs at my question, "Yes, you can tell your lover boy."

I smile and give her another hug. The announcement came up, signaling the ceremony is about to start.

After the children, and pre-teen went it was my class's turn. We did a short little performance that was lighthearted and funny, earning slight laughter from the crowd.

I frowned slightly when I noticed that Azrail wasn't present but that changed when he and Jason rushed in causing a bit of a ruckus. I looked over at Rosalie who was trying hard to hold in her laugh.

The boys look like they ran from the tattoo shop to the building, Azrail frowning at Jason who undoubtedly was the reason for their lateness.

After our performances it was time for prizes and presentations, those went by slowly. Coach called out my name and the other dancers who were moving up, gave us a trophy and made a speech about how proud she is of us and how far we will go. I got a few medals for accomplishments I didn't even know I achieved, the coach's words left us in tears.

"You were amazing, my sweet child," Dad said, pulling me into a hug when the ceremony was done. My mom joined in.

"Daddy, Ma, I can't breathe." I cough, pulling away from their bear hugs.

Azrail who was standing behind them came up and gave me a hug once they let me go.

"You were amazing Sunshine,"

"Thank you turtle,"

"Sorry for making us late, he wouldn't sit still for his tattoo," Jason says, coming up to us, Rosalie on his arm.

Azrail rolls his eyes, "You were just being slow."

"You got new tattoos?" I examined Azrail trying to see if I noticed any new ink.

"Mainly on my chest and back, I'll show you later." He says winking at me.

Our moment was cut short by my mom's awkward cough, "Aisha make sure you get home by eleven."

A curfew? Since when?

"Yes ma'am."

"Some family are coming over tonight, I want you to greet them before they go to bed."

I nod.

"We got to pick them up from the airport in two hours, good job again sweetie." My dad says giving me a final hug and saying goodbye. I wave by to my parents and focus on Azrail.

"What's next?"

"Shower, change, and then date." He says give me a peck. I bid goodbye to everyone and made my way to Azrail's car.

"This is nice," I commented walking into the restaurant that Azrail picked for our date. It was a nice Italian restaurant, classical music playing in the background, we were definitely the youngest customers there.

"Only the best for my Sunshine," he comments, pulling the chair for me to sit down.

God, I hope he's not proposing.

I think about looking around the restaurant. I do want to marry him but I haven't even started college yet, we are way too young.

"I know that look," He says, pulling me out of my thoughts. "I'm not proposing, don't worry."

"Oh," I mutter a bit embarrassed.

"I want to marry you but let's wait till our frontal lobe develops," He says, putting his hand on me. "Now open your gift."

I take the box and open it. It was a beautiful gold necklace with a sun pendant attached to it.

"Wow," I muttered looking at the necklace. It was simply gorgeous.

"I was going to get you a necklace with my name in it but I thought that was too much, so I got you the meaning instead."

"When did Azrail mean 'sun'?"

"It doesn't, Asahi does though," He corrects. "Morning sun to be exact."

I sigh looking deep into his eyes.

My perfect boy.

"I'm so glad I met you,"

"Same to you my love,"

Epilogue

AISHA

TUESDAY

"It is hot as hell in this motherfucker," Jamila comments, making me laugh.

It's graduation day, Jamila and I sat next to each other since our last names are the same, funny enough. Unfortunately, our last name made us one of the last people to be called for our diplomas.

We were stuck watching everyone get their diplomas, sitting underneath the fan and getting a nice breeze, not looking like a sweating mess.

"This is one of the moments where I'm thankful for my condition," I comment, getting a glare from a sweating Jamila.

"Lucky bitch,"

"Love you too."

"How much longer," She wines.

"They just started calling out names, we will be done soon."

"Azrail Morris"

"THAT'S MY BABYYYYYYYYYYYYYY,"

"THAT'S MY BABY'S BABYYYY"

"THAT'S MY MAN"

"THAT'S MY BEST FRIEND."

"WOOOOOOOOOOOOOOOOOOOOOOOOOOOOOOO"

The shouts from our family, friends, and I earned some laughter in the crowd. I watch as Azrail scurries through the stage. I was too far to see his face, but I know for a fact he was turning red.

"He's gonna get you for that," Jamila comments, laughing at me.

"I wasn't the only one,"

"But he made you promise," She says and I shrug not feeling shame for my action. I was proud of my man, and I'm going to flaunt it.

Soon enough it was time for my row to go up, I looked in the crowd as my family prepared themselves to make a big commotion.

"Aisha Wyatt."

I walk across the stage as my family and friends make a big commotion, making me smile. I noticed my mom crying in the crowd and the principal had to stop, waiting for silence before calling Jamila's name, which also gained the same reaction.

So much for waiting till the end for applause.

※　※

3 MONTHS LATER

"I can't believe my baby is moving out," Mom cries out giving me a big hug, crying in the middle of my dorm.

"Mom, you and Daddy literally moved twenty minutes away, you will see me," I comment, rolling my eyes playfully.

"Do you have to be in a dorm?" Dad asks, looking at the dorm with the most disgusting look on his face.

"Mandatory for first and second-year students," I half lied. I did have the option to opt-out if my guardian lived close enough, but I wanted a bit of freedom.

I mean yes my parents do give me that freedom and I usually spend most of my time alone at home, but now that they have been more active in my life, something I'm not used to. I started to feel suffocated, and I wanted the college experience.

"You're coming over tomorrow for dinner right?" Mom asks.

"Yeah I'll be there, can I bring Azrail? He's all alone." I ask, although his family is well off, Mrs. Morris doesn't have the privilege to just up and move like my parents do. She has to stay in the hospital.

"Of course, how was his move-in?"

"I'm not sure, I haven't had time to talk to him today."

Azrail moved into his dorm two days before I did, so we haven't had time to actually talk because of the packing and student orientation he had to attend.

"This shouldn't be legal," My dad comments while looking around my dorm. "I'll contact the school about this, you could get sick."

I laugh at his micromanaging.

"Daddy, I promise if something happens and I feel uncomfortable in my dorm, I'll contact you right away," I responded, giving him a hug. "Now go and explore the city with Mom, I need to unpack and make this room nice before my roommates move in tomorrow."

We bid our farewell and I went straight to cleaning and rearranging my stuff. I was lucky enough to be put in a dorm that has rooms and two bathrooms. I was also lucky enough to move in first and get the single room closest to the bathroom. Unfortunately, I had four other roommates to deal with and I barely knew them. That's the dorm life I guess.

Time passed and I was almost done with my dorm, just a few stuff I needed to be built but didn't want to call my dad to do it for me. I pulled out my phone to look up how-to videos on youtube when I noticed two missed calls from Azrail.

I was so busy cleaning I didn't hear the phone ringing.

"You remember me."

I laugh at his fake winning. "Sorry turtle, I was cleaning and didn't hear my phone ring."

"It's alright Sunshine, how are you enjoying dorm life?"

"It hasn't set in yet, I like my room though, I don't know how I'm going to get along with my four roommates. I wish I only had one like you,"

"No, you don't, it's hell, only one shared space, and communal bathroom."

I cringe at that, shaking my head.

"I take my wish back, I'm sorry turtle."

"I'll live," he says. "Plus, I live in the same city as my girl-friend, life is good."

"I can't wait to see y-"

Knock. Knock.

"Hold up turtle, someone is at my dorm."

I walk out of the bathroom and make my way to the front door, ready to introduce myself to another freshman that's moving in on my floor.

"Surprise,"

"What are you doing here?" I squeal jumping on an off-guard Azrail, making him stumble before he wraps his arms around me

"I don't think I could have waited another day to see you Sunshine, I missed you." He says hands still wrapped tightly around my waist as he walked into the dorm, closing the door behind him.

"I miss you too," I mutter, pulling him for a kiss.

"How did you manage to get in?" I asked, pulling away from the kiss.

"Doors are open and people are going in and out today so I managed to sneak in," He explains. "I'm sure it'll be much stricter when the moving day is done."

I sit on my bed and watch him look around my room. The pictures of us that I printed out, and the drawings he's given to me caught his attention.

"These pictures are new," he asked, pointing at a picture of us sleeping together.

"Your mom took it and sent it to me," I mentioned walking to him and staring at the picture. "It's one of my favorites. Remember when we first started cuddling with each other."

He nods, "With you by my side, I felt like a brand new person."

"I'm grateful for that accidental first touch," I comment. "The touch that led to our beautiful friendship and romance."

"Remember our first kiss?"

I blush at his questions, of course I remember.

"I remember your words, something like *touch me Sunshine*" I start off looking up at him.

"You're the only one who can." He finishes before pulling me into a deep kiss.

Coming Soon

Teach Me

February 2026

Heal Me

TBD

Teach Me

TEASER

JAMES

Knock. Knock.

"Come in,"

The door to my office opens slowly, I watch my wife walk with two glasses of whiskey in her hand. She gives me a small smile, sitting on my lap without an invitation.

Not that she needed one.

Taking the whiskey from her hand, I take a sip and kiss her on the lip. Her presence brings me peace.

"Are you stalking our daughter again?"

I shrug, watching the security camera in the location Aisha is having her prom in. She and that boyfriend of hers were currently dancing to a slow song.

"I don't like him." I mutter, glaring at the boy through the screen.

"Liar," My wife teases, laying her head on my chest. "Do I need to ask you about the sudden death of that officer who arrested him?"

"Heart attack."

"Or why it was so easy to change his name on his birth certificate and seal of his record?"

"I don't know what you're talking about."

She laughs at that, "Deny all you want but I know you like that boy. If you didn't, he and Aisha wouldn't be together, no matter how much she fought you on that."

"I think you're wrong Daisy,"

She cocks a brow at my words, I don't tell her she's wrong often.

"The way our little princess acted when he was in the hospital, I wouldn't be surprised if she left us behind for him. She loves him."

She stays silent for a bit before nodding, "Like father, like daughter."

With that we stay quiet, me nursing my whiskey, while Daisy lays on me, both of us watching our daughter enjoying her last few days of high school. As Daisy falls asleep on me, and the dance ends, I click on another file on the computer, a slideshow of pictures starting.

I let my mind wander to the past, when a certain klutz spilled coffee on me the day of her interview. That same klutz that taught me how to feel.

Teach Me: The story of Aisha's parents, Daisy and James. Out February 2026.

About the Author

AB Monnette, was born in Port-au-Prince, Haiti and immigrated to the U.S. at a young age. Her passion for reading and writing have been present for as long as she can remember. She loves romance, and as a reader who did not see a lot of people that looked like her she decided to take matters into her own hands and start writing the fantasies she wants.

A.B started writing on Wattpad at 15 years old, but took a break for school and mental health. In 2020, during the quarantine she went back to writing, having over 6 novels published on Wattpad. She is currently on the search for a literary agent, but as she waits, she decide to bring her work out to the public through self-publishing. She edits her own works and hopes that one day, her platform can grow and she can become like one of the many authors she admires.

Wattpad: https://www.wattpad.com/user/AB_Monnette
Instagram: https://www.instagram.com/ab.monnette/